the spoiled duke

TRISHA FUENTES

The Spoiled Duke
Copyright © 2024 by Trisha Fuentes
All rights reserved.

Book Cover and formatting provided by Trisha Fuentes
https://bit.ly/m/trishafuentes

No part of this book may be reproduced in any form or by any electronic or mechanical means, including information storage and retrieval systems, without written permission from the author, except for the use of brief quotations in a book review.

ISBN: 979-8-3306-1720-3 (Paperback)

Published by
Ardent Artist Books
www.ardentartistbooks.com

about ardent artist books

➥ ABOUT US

Ardent Artist Books was established in 2008

We publish modern and historical romances once a month!

Get Your FREE List: Published & Upcoming Books
visit our website at:
https://bit.ly/3Wva4o0

➥ WE HAVE BOOK TRAILERS TOO!

Follow us on YouTube!
https://bit.ly/3W3xn7a

Like, Subscribe & Comment

➥ READ SERIALIZED FICTION!

Visit our website today to download one of our stories that unfold in bite-sized pieces!

Each installment is just 99¢!

https://bit.ly/3LsDpJL

➥ LET'S CONNECT!

Fuel your love of fiction with exclusive content and captivating insights from Ardent Artist Books. Whether you crave the thrill of modern narratives or the timeless elegance of historical fiction, our newsletter delivers a curated selection straight to your inbox. Plus, as a welcome gift, receive a FREE downloadable eBook:

"The Family Fix"
https://bit.ly/49BR3UB

contents

1. A Dangerous Reputation — 1
2. Arriving at Blackwood Estate — 11
3. An Electric Encounter — 21
4. Unexpected Encounters — 33
5. A Moment of Weakness — 47
6. The Butterfly — 57
7. Whispers of Scandal — 71
8. The Dismissal — 85
9. Revelations — 97
10. A New Role — 107
11. The Fair at Hyde Park — 119
12. Spoiled No More — 127
13. News Beyond These Walls — 141
    Epilogue — 151

You Might Also Like — 165
Best-Seller! — 167
One Starry Night — 169
About Trisha — 171
Also by Trisha Fuentes — 173

CHAPTER ONE
a dangerous reputation

The candlelight from a thousand glittering chandeliers cast golden shadows across the ballroom of Lord Ashworth's London townhouse. Beneath their glow, the cream of society whirled and twirled in an endless dance of silk and scandal. At the center of it all stood the Duke of Blackwood, Edward Ashcombe, commanding attention without effort.

"Have you heard?" Lady Pembrook whispered behind her fan to her companion. "They say he broke poor Miss Fairfax's heart last season."

"Better a broken heart than a broken reputation," her friend replied with a knowing look.

The Duke cut an imposing figure as he moved through the crowd, his broad shoulders draped in perfectly tailored black evening wear that only emphasized the intensity of his azure gaze. A lock of raven hair fell carelessly across his forehead, lending him a rakish air that had young debutantes swooning in his wake.

"My Elizabeth would make him the perfect duchess," Lady

Rutherford declared to her circle of confidantes. "She has such a steady temperament."

"As did Miss Fairfax, and look where that led," came the dry response.

Edward's lips curved into a practiced smile as he bowed over yet another young lady's hand. The gesture was perfect, the words were charming, but his eyes remained distant. He had played this game too many times before. He watched the endless parade of eligible young ladies with growing weariness, though his practiced smile never wavered. The orchestra had struck up another country dance, and he found himself partnered with Lady Elizabeth Rutherford, who gazed up at him with undisguised admiration.

"Your Grace, you dance divinely," she simpered, her steps perfectly executed but lacking any real spirit.

"You are too kind, Lady Elizabeth." The words fell from his lips automatically, as hollow as the compliments he'd bestowed upon countless others before her.

As they moved through the intricate steps, Edward's mind wandered to the peculiar emptiness that seemed to grow with each passing season. *Freedom* - that's what he told himself he cherished most. The ability to come and go as he pleased, to drive his curricle at breakneck speeds through Hyde Park, to stay out until dawn at his club without answering to anyone. No wife to demand his attention or question his choices.

And yet...

"I trust you'll attend Lady Pembroke's garden party next week?" Lady Elizabeth's voice cut through his reverie.

"Perhaps." He executed a perfect turn. "Though I find my calendar rather full these days."

The dance ended, and Edward bowed over Lady Elizabeth's hand before escaping to the edges of the ballroom. He caught his reflection in one of the gilt-framed mirrors - impeccably dressed, not a hair out of place despite the evening's exertions. The very image of a proper duke, save for that persistent gleam of restlessness in his eyes.

Love.

Such a small word for something that seemed to hold such power over others. He'd watched his friends succumb one by one, transformed from carefree bachelors into devoted husbands. Even his rakish cousin John, who'd sworn never to be caught in parson's mousetrap, had fallen headlong for a country miss with spectacles and ink-stained fingers.

"Another glass of champagne, Your Grace?" A footman appeared at his elbow with a laden tray.

Edward took a crystal flute, though the golden liquid had lost its appeal hours ago. He'd seen what people called love - in poetry, in novels, in the faces of newly wedded couples. *But was it real? Or merely an elaborate fiction designed to trap unsuspecting souls into the prison of matrimony?*

"Your Grace!" Lady Pembrook's shrill voice carried across the room. "Do come and meet my niece - she's just arrived from Bath!"

Edward's lips curved into that familiar, meaningless smile as he made his way toward yet another introduction. If love existed - true love, not this elaborate dance of fortune-hunting and social climbing - surely he would have encountered it by now. Perhaps it was like those mythical creatures in his niece Beatrice's storybooks - beautiful to imagine but existing only in fancy.

Still, he could not deny the growing curiosity. *What would it feel like to look at someone and see more than just a pretty face or an advantageous connection? To feel something genuine stir beneath the carefully maintained facade of ducal propriety?*

Until he found that answer, he would continue this masquerade. Let them whisper behind their fans about the notorious Duke of Blackwood. Let them scheme and plot to capture his title, his fortune, his hand. He would smile and bow and dance, all the while searching for that elusive spark that had transformed so many of his acquaintances from mere mortals into love's willing slaves.

The evening wore on, and Edward performed his role to perfection. Each laugh, each gallant phrase, each perfectly executed dance step drew admiring glances and hopeful sighs. Yet beneath it all, that nagging question remained: was love truly a myth, or was he simply unable to recognize it when it appeared before him?

Edward found himself cornered by yet another ambitious mama, this time the formidable Lady Winchester, who practically thrust her daughter forward like a prized offering at the altar.

"Your Grace, might I present my daughter, Miss Penelope Winchester." Lady Winchester's eyes gleamed with calculation as she watched the Duke bow over her daughter's delicate hand.

Miss Penelope was a vision in pale pink silk, her golden curls arranged in the latest fashion, though her cheeks flushed an unfashionable shade of red at the Duke's attention. She could not have been more than seventeen - fresh from the schoolroom and utterly unprepared for the likes of him.

"Miss Winchester," Edward's voice held just the right note of appreciation. "I trust you are enjoying your first Season?"

"Oh! Yes, Your Grace," she twisted her fingers in her fan, her eyes downcast. "Though I find London rather overwhelming at times."

"Such charming modesty," Lady Winchester interjected, her dark eyes fixed upon Edward with an intensity that made him take particular notice. Unlike her daughter's nervous fidgeting, Lady Winchester possessed the kind of confidence that came with years of navigating society's treacherous waters. "Penelope has been thoroughly educated in all the accomplishments a young lady requires."

"Indeed?" Edward maintained his focus on the daughter, though he found himself increasingly aware of the mother's presence. Lady Winchester wore a gown of deep burgundy that complemented her mature beauty, and there was something compelling about the way she carried herself - a grace that spoke of experience rather than training.

"I... I play the pianoforte," Miss Penelope offered timidly.

"Beautifully," her mother added. "And she paints watercolors with remarkable skill."

Edward performed the expected courtesies, requesting the pleasure of Miss Penelope's hand for the next set. As they took their places in the formation, he could not help but notice how Lady Winchester watched their every move, her lips curved in a smile that held secrets her daughter had yet to learn.

The dance began, and Miss Penelope proved to be a capable partner, though her conversation consisted mainly of one-word answers and nervous glances at her feet. Edward guided her through the steps with practiced ease, offering gentle encouragement when she faltered.

"You must find these affairs rather tedious," he ventured, attempting to draw her out.

"Oh no, Your Grace! That is... I mean... they are quite exciting." Her words tumbled out in a rush of youthful enthusiasm.

But Edward's attention had already wandered back to Lady Winchester, who stood at the edge of the ballroom engaged in animated conversation with Lady Rutherford. There was something utterly captivating about the way she gestured, the elegant arch of her neck, the knowing glint in her eye when she caught him watching her.

The dance ended, and Edward returned Miss Penelope to her mother with impeccable manners. "Your daughter dances beautifully, Lady Winchester. You must be very proud."

"She has had excellent instruction," Lady Winchester's voice held a note of amusement, as though she understood perfectly well that his compliment was mere politeness. "Though I confess, I was quite the accomplished dancer myself in my day."

"Your day?" Edward raised an eyebrow. "Surely you still frequent the dance floor, my lady?"

A becoming flush colored Lady Winchester's cheeks. "Your Grace is too kind. But I leave such vigorous pursuits to the young these days."

"A great pity," Edward's voice dropped lower, meant for her ears alone. "I should very much like to test that claim of accomplished dancing."

Miss Penelope stood forgotten between them, her young face a study in confusion as she watched this subtle exchange. Lady Winchester's fan moved with deliberate slowness, creating a brief moment of privacy.

"Perhaps another time, Your Grace," Her eyes met his over the top of her fan. "When there are fewer... observers."

Edward felt a thrill of anticipation that had nothing to do with the innocent miss still standing before them. Here was a woman who understood the game they all played, who knew the steps of this dance far better than her daughter ever could.

Lady Winchester turned her attention back to her daughter, effectively dismissing him. "Come, Penelope dear. I believe Lady Rutherford wished to introduce you to her nephew."

ACROSS THE ROOM, Lady Helena Epworth watched her brother with a furrowed brow. "I fear he grows worse with each passing season," she confided to Lady Margaret, her closest friend since childhood. "The drinking, the gambling, the endless stream of broken hearts - it cannot continue."

"He is still young," Lady Margaret offered gently. "Perhaps he merely needs the right influence."

"Young?" Helena laughed. "He will be thirty next month."

Lady Margaret pretended to gasp, "Still young, why my Harold proposed to me when he turned thirty-two."

Helena's gloved fingers worried at her necklace. "I cannot help but think of Beatrice. What future will she have if her uncle's reputation continues to decline? Already I hear whispers when I enter a room - *the poor widow*, they say, living under the protection of such a man."

Helena's fingers traced the delicate pearl pendant at her throat - a gift from her late husband on their first wedding anniversary. "I worry for Beatrice most of all. She needs guidance, structure... a father figure." Her voice caught on the last words.

"Your brother does cut quite the figure in society," Lady Margaret acknowledged, watching Edward charm yet another young debutante. "Though perhaps not the sort one wishes to emulate."

"Last week, I found him teaching her how to play cards," Helena's lips pressed into a thin line. "Cards, Margaret. She's but five years old."

"Well, at least he didn't teach her his betting system," Lady Margaret paused at Helena's stricken expression. "He didn't, did he?"

"The very same day," Helena's shoulders slumped. "Oh, how George would have handled it all so differently. He would have read to her, taught her about the flowers in the garden, shown her the constellations in the night sky..."

The orchestra struck up another lively tune, but Helena barely noticed, lost in memories of quieter, happier times. "Sometimes in the evenings, when the house grows still, I catch myself listening for his footsteps in the hall. Foolish, isn't it? Three years gone, and still..."

Lady Margaret covered Helena's hand with her own. "Not foolish at all, dearest. Though perhaps... have you considered that Beatrice might benefit from a more structured education? Someone to guide her daily lessons?"

"We've interviewed countless governesses," Helena sighed. "Edward finds fault with each one. Too stern, too lax, too young, too old. I begin to think he objects merely for the sport of it."

"Ah!" Lady Margaret's eyes brightened. "Then I may have the perfect solution. Are you familiar with Miss Charlotte Larkspur?"

Helena shook her head.

"She's currently with the Pembroke family, though I understand her position there is coming to an end - young Alfred is off to Eton this autumn. She's absolutely marvelous with children. Quick-witted, patient, and possessed of the most serene temperament I've ever encountered."

"Edward would surely find some fault—"

"Let me write to her directly," Lady Margaret interrupted. "I'll invite her to Blackwood Estate myself. Once your brother sees how she interacts with Beatrice, he can hardly object."

"You seem quite certain of this Miss Larkspur's qualities."

"My dear Helena, when have I ever steered you wrong?" Lady Margaret's eyes twinkled. "Besides, the woman practically worked miracles with young Alfred Pembroke. That boy was positively feral before she took him in hand - now he can recite Shakespeare and knows which fork to use at dinner."

"Beatrice isn't feral," Helena protested, though a smile tugged at her lips.

"No, but she could use a steady hand to guide her. Someone who understands that a young lady needs more than card tricks and betting systems in her education."

Helena glanced across the room where Edward now lounged against a pillar, a glass of brandy in hand. "You'll write to her soon?"

"First thing tomorrow," Lady Margaret promised. "Trust me, Helena. Miss Larkspur may be exactly what Blackwood Estate needs."

CHAPTER TWO
arriving at blackwood estate

The late afternoon sun cast long shadows across the immaculate grounds of Blackwood Estate as Charlotte Larkspur's carriage rolled to a stop before the grand manor house. Her breath caught at the sight of the pale stone façade, its graceful lines stretching toward the azure sky. Ornate carvings adorned the windows and doorways, while stately pillars flanked the entrance. The gardens sprawled in every direction, a tapestry of vibrant blooms and manicured hedgerows that spoke of meticulous care and generations of wealth.

Charlotte smoothed her gray traveling dress, acutely aware of its modest quality against such opulent surroundings. A footman assisted her descent from the carriage, and she clutched her small reticule close, her heart fluttering with equal parts anticipation and trepidation. The weight of responsibility settled upon her shoulders – this position as governess to Lady Helena's daughter could secure her future, yet the prospect of navigating life among the nobility filled her with unease.

The massive oak doors swung open, revealing a grand entrance hall that took Charlotte's breath away. Crystal chandeliers cast dancing lights across marble floors, while ancestral portraits gazed down from gilded frames, their eyes seeming to follow her progress across the polished expanse.

A butler led her to an elegantly appointed drawing room where Lady Helena Epworth awaited. The young widow rose from her seat, her black mourning dress a stark contrast to the pastel-hued furnishings. Despite the obvious signs of fatigue around her eyes, Helena's smile was genuine and warm.

"Miss Larkspur, welcome to Blackwood Estate," Lady Helena gestured to a nearby chair. "Please, be seated."

Lady Helena studied the young woman before her, noting how Charlotte's chestnut waves caught the afternoon light streaming through the tall windows. There was something compelling about her quiet grace, the way she held herself with dignity despite her station. Her hazel eyes sparkled with intelligence, and the modest gray dress, while plain, suited her slim figure and spoke of practical sensibility.

"Your references from the Pembroke family are most impressive," Helena's fingers traced the edge of the letter on the side table, her heart constricting at the thought of entrusting Beatrice to another's care. "They speak highly of your dedication to their children's education."

Charlotte's hands were folded neatly in her lap, her posture impeccable yet not rigid. "The Pembroke children were a joy to teach, my lady. I found great fulfillment in nurturing their minds and spirits."

Helena rose and walked to the window, gazing out at the gardens where Beatrice often played. The weight of her decisions pressed heavily upon her shoulders. Since George's death, she had struggled to maintain the delicate balance between mourning wife and present mother. The endless nights of holding her sobbing daughter, of trying to explain why Papa would never return, had taken their toll.

"My Beatrice is…" Helena paused, searching for the right words. "She is a sensitive child. The loss of her father has affected her deeply." She turned back to face Charlotte, studying the young woman's expression for any hint of hesitation or judgment.

"I understand the gravity of such circumstances, my lady." Charlotte's voice carried a note of genuine empathy that touched Helena's heart. "Children process grief differently than adults, and each requires a unique approach to healing."

The grandfather clock in the corner marked the passing seconds with solemn precision as Helena wrestled with her inner turmoil. She had promised George she would give Beatrice every advantage, every opportunity to grow into a proper lady of society. Yet the thought of sharing her daughter's precious childhood years with another caused an ache in her chest.

"I confess, Miss Larkspur, I had not planned to engage a governess so soon," Helena sank back into her chair, her fingers worrying at the black fabric of her dress. "But circumstances…" She thought of her brother's increasing notoriety, the whispers at social gatherings, the pitying glances from other mothers. "Circumstances have made it necessary to ensure Beatrice receives proper guidance and education."

Charlotte leaned forward slightly, her expression earnest. "If I may speak freely, my lady?"

Helena nodded, curious.

"A mother's love cannot be replaced or replicated. My role, should you choose to entrust me with it, would be to complement your guidance, not to supersede it."

The words settled in Helena's chest like a warm balm. She observed how the sunlight caught the subtle auburn highlights in Charlotte's hair, the gentle determination in her bearing. There was something refreshingly honest about her presence, a quality that seemed rare in their social circle of carefully crafted appearances and veiled meanings.

"Tell me, Miss Larkspur, what do you consider most vital in a child's education?"

"Character, my lady. While accomplishments in music, art, and languages are important, I believe nurturing a child's heart and mind takes precedence. Teaching them to think critically, to show compassion, to face challenges with courage – these are the foundations upon which all other learning must rest."

Helena's breath caught. These were the very values she and George had discussed during those precious quiet moments before his passing. She could almost hear his voice: *"Our Beatrice must learn to be strong, my love. The world will not always be kind."*

A sound of childish laughter drifted through the window, and Helena turned to see Beatrice chasing butterflies in the garden below, her dark curls bouncing with each step. The sight both warmed and wounded her heart. Her daughter needed more than a grieving mother could provide alone – she needed structure, guidance, and fresh energy to help her navigate the path ahead.

CHARLOTTE STUDIED Lady Helena's delicate features, noting how grief had left its subtle marks upon her beauty. The young widow's raven hair fell in gentle waves past her shoulders, partially concealed by the black lace cap that marked her mourning status. Her blue eyes, though touched by sorrow, retained a warmth that spoke of inner strength. Despite her petite frame and the shadow of fatigue that clung to her, she carried herself with quiet dignity.

Watching Lady Helena gaze at her daughter through the window stirred something profound in Charlotte's heart. Here was a woman barely older than herself, thrust into the crushing weight of single motherhood through tragedy rather than choice. The pain of such a loss seemed etched in every careful movement, every measured word.

"My lady, might I ask about Beatrice's current interests?" Charlotte kept her tone gentle, hoping to draw Lady Helena's thoughts toward happier contemplations. The slight tremor in the widow's hands as she smoothed her skirts had not escaped Charlotte's notice.

Lady Helena's face softened at the mention of her daughter. "She adores stories, particularly tales of fairies and magical gardens. George used to..." She faltered, her composure wavering for just a moment before she recovered. "My husband would create the most wonderful adventures for her."

The raw emotion in those words struck Charlotte deeply. *How many nights had this young mother lain awake, wondering how to fill the void left by her husband's passing? How does one preserve such precious memories while helping a child move forward?*

"She has his eyes," Lady Helena continued, almost to herself. "Sometimes when she laughs, I hear echoes of him."

Charlotte's chest tightened with empathy. She thought of her own losses - different in nature but no less profound - and how they had shaped her understanding of grief's many faces. "Such memories are precious gifts, my lady. They keep love alive in the most beautiful ways."

The grandfather clock's steady ticking filled the silence that followed, each second marked by the weight of shared understanding. Through the window, Beatrice's laughter floated up again, a bright counterpoint to the solemnity of the moment.

Charlotte observed how Lady Helena's fingers unconsciously traced the black band on her wrist, a gesture that spoke volumes about the battles she fought daily between duty and despair. Despite her youth - she couldn't be more than twenty-eight - responsibility had settled heavily upon her shoulders. Yet there was something admirable in how she carried it, in her determination to secure the best future for her daughter.

"I believe," Charlotte ventured carefully, "that children often show us the path through our darkest moments. Their capacity for joy, even in the midst of sorrow, can be quite remarkable."

Lady Helena turned from the window, her blue eyes meeting Charlotte's with sudden intensity. "You speak as one who understands loss, Miss Larkspur."

"I have known its touch, yes," Charlotte acknowledged, thinking of the circumstances that had led her to seek employment as a governess. "Though my experiences pale in comparison to yours, my lady."

"Pain is not a competition," Lady Helena replied softly. "It shapes us all differently."

The afternoon sun caught the subtle sheen of tears in Lady Helena's eyes, though none fell. Charlotte marveled at her composure, the way she balanced vulnerability with strength. Here was a woman who had faced society's pitying glances and whispered sympathies, yet maintained her dignity throughout.

"Would you like to meet Beatrice?" Lady Helena asked, her voice steadying as she rose from her chair. The question carried weight beyond its simple words - it was an offering of trust, a tentative step toward allowing another person into their closely guarded world.

Charlotte's heart swelled with both anticipation and responsibility. "I would be honored, my lady."

Just as they got up from their seated positions, a burst of childish laughter interrupted their silence as the door flew open. A small whirlwind in pale blue muslin bounded into the room, dark curls bouncing with each step. "Mama! Jasper says the cherry tarts are ready!"

"Beatrice," Lady Helena chided gently, though her eyes sparkled with affection. "What have I said about bursting into rooms unannounced?"

The child ducked her head, though her smile remained irrepressible. "That it isn't ladylike behavior." Her gaze shifted to Charlotte, curiosity lighting her features. "Who are you?"

"This is Miss Larkspur," Helena explained. "She may become your new governess."

Beatrice's face brightened. "Do you know any stories about fairies? My last governess only told boring stories about proper young ladies."

Charlotte leaned forward conspiratorially. "As it happens, I know several tales about fairy courts hidden in garden roses. Would you like to hear one?"

"Oh, yes please!" Beatrice clapped her hands in delight.

Before Charlotte could begin, heavy footsteps echoed in the hallway. The drawing room door swung open once more, revealing a tall figure whose very presence seemed to alter the atmosphere of the room. The Duke of Blackwood stood framed in the doorway, his striking features set in lines of aristocratic hauteur. His azure eyes swept the room, lingering on Charlotte with an intensity that sent a shiver down her spine.

"Brother," Helena said, rising. "Allow me to present Miss Charlotte Larkspur. She comes highly recommended as a governess for Beatrice."

The Duke's penetrating gaze never left Charlotte's face as he advanced into the room.

The air in the drawing room crackled with unforeseen tension as the Duke of Blackwood's azure eyes met Charlotte's hazel eyes. His initial dismissive glance transformed into something deeper, more searching, as he took in her steadfast composure. The customary smirk that graced his features—the one that had broken countless hearts across London's ballrooms—faltered for the briefest moment.

"So, you are to be my niece's new governess," his voice carried the rich timbre of authority, yet beneath it lay an unmistakable note of curiosity.

"Indeed, Your Grace," Charlotte executed a perfect curtsy, her movements fluid and graceful. "If Lady Helena deems me suitable for the position."

"Come now, surely you must have grander aspirations than teaching a child her letters?"

"I find no greater aspiration than shaping a young mind, Your Grace. Though perhaps you consider such pursuits beneath notice?"

The Duke's eyebrows rose at her gentle riposte. He took two measured steps closer, his tall frame casting a shadow across the Turkish carpet. "Helena, Beatrice, leave us. I wish to speak with Miss Larkspur alone."

Lady Helena opened her mouth as if to protest, but something in her brother's expression made her pause. She gathered Beatrice, who was engrossed in arranging her dolls by the window seat, and departed with a concerned glance over her shoulder.

The Duke gestated to a nearby chair. "Please, sit."

Charlotte lowered herself onto the edge of the seat, her back straight as a board, while the Duke claimed the adjacent armchair, stretching his long legs before him with casual elegance.

CHAPTER THREE
an electric encounter

Edward's gaze traced the gentle curves of Charlotte's figure, noting the way her modest gown did little to hide her natural grace. The sunlight streaming through the window caught the auburn highlights in her chestnut hair, and for a moment, he found himself wondering how it might feel beneath his fingers. He shifted in his chair, attempting to quell the unexpected surge of attraction that coursed through him.

"Tell me, Miss Larkspur, what experience do you have with children?" His voice emerged harder than intended, a defensive mechanism against his own unsettling thoughts.

"I have taught at Mrs. Weatherby's School for Young Ladies for the past three years, Your Grace." Charlotte's fingers smoothed an invisible wrinkle from her skirts, the gesture betraying a hint of nervousness beneath her composed exterior.

Edward forced his attention to the bookshelf beyond her shoulder, fighting the urge to study the way her throat moved as she spoke. *This would not do at all.* A governess living under his roof, particularly one who stirred such immediate interest, could only lead to complications.

"And you find such work fulfilling?" He kept his tone deliberately dismissive, though his pulse quickened when she lifted her chin in response.

"More than fulfilling, Your Grace. Each child possesses unique gifts waiting to be discovered and nurtured."

The earnestness in her voice drew his eyes back to her face. Blast it all, even her modest demeanor held an allure he hadn't encountered in the painted and powdered ladies of the ton. He rose abruptly, needing distance between them.

"My sister seems convinced of your capabilities," he moved to the window, clasping his hands behind his back. "Though I must warn you, Miss Larkspur, Beatrice can be rather... spirited."

"The most spirited children often possess the keenest minds, Your Grace."

Edward's lips twitched at her diplomatic response. He could feel her presence behind him like a physical touch, making his shoulders tense. What devil had possessed Helena to hire a governess who combined intelligence with beauty in such a dangerous measure?

CHARLOTTE'S HEART fluttered traitorously as the Duke's broad shoulders filled her vision. The afternoon sunlight streaming through the window cast him in a golden glow, highlighting the strong line of his jaw and the subtle disarray of his raven hair. She pressed her palms flat against her skirts, willing them to stop trembling.

Lord above, what is wrong with me? She had encountered plenty of handsome men during her years of teaching - dashing fathers and brothers who made other governesses swoon and giggle behind their fans. Yet none had affected her quite like this. The Duke of Blackwood's mere presence seemed to draw the very air from her lungs.

"Do you play the pianoforte, Miss Larkspur?" The Duke turned suddenly, catching her studying him. A knowing glint appeared in those striking blue eyes.

"I do, Your Grace, though I confess I am merely proficient rather than accomplished." Charlotte fought to keep her voice steady as he stepped closer. The scent of sandalwood and leather enveloped her, making it difficult to maintain her composure.

"Perhaps you might demonstrate for us one evening. Beatrice is quite fond of music."

Demonstrate? While he watches? The thought of performing under that intense gaze sent a shiver down her spine that had nothing to do with fear. "If Lady Helena wishes it, of course."

Edward moved closer still, ostensibly to examine a small portrait on the wall beside her chair. Charlotte held her breath as his arm brushed against her shoulder. Heat bloomed wherever their bodies made contact, however briefly.

This is madness, she thought desperately. *He is my employer's brother, a duke far above my station. I cannot entertain such improper thoughts.*

Yet her traitorous mind conjured images of those elegant fingers caressing her cheek instead of the portrait's frame. Of his lips, currently curved in that devastating half-smile, pressed against her own. Charlotte shot to her feet, nearly stumbling in her haste to put distance between them.

"Are you quite well, Miss Larkspur?" The Duke's voice held a note of concern, though his eyes sparkled with something that looked suspiciously like satisfaction at her obvious discomfort.

"Perfectly well, Your Grace. I merely thought I heard Beatrice calling." The lie fell awkwardly from her lips. She needed to escape before she did something foolish - like reaching out to smooth that wayward lock of hair that had fallen across his forehead.

"I heard nothing." He tilted his head, studying her with the intensity of a hunting hawk. "Though perhaps your hearing is more acute than mine."

Charlotte's cheeks burned under his scrutiny. The pull between them was almost tangible now, like invisible threads drawing them together. She had never experienced anything like it - this visceral awareness of another person that seemed to bypass all reason and propriety.

I must keep my distance, she resolved firmly. *The position of governess requires dignity and discretion. I cannot risk everything I've worked for because of some... some inconvenient attraction.*

"If you'll excuse me, Your Grace, I should find Lady Helena to discuss Beatrice's schedule." Charlotte dipped into another curtsy, proud that she managed it without wobbling despite her weak knees.

"By all means." Edward's voice had dropped to a low purr that seemed to caress her very skin. "Though I suspect we'll be seeing quite a lot of each other, Miss Larkspur. Blackwood Estate isn't nearly as large as it appears."

Charlotte fled - there was no other word for it - from the drawing room, her pulse racing and her thoughts in chaos. *How was she to maintain her professional demeanor when every fiber of her being seemed to recognize something in the Duke that called to her very soul?*

Distance, she reminded herself firmly as she hurried down the corridor. She would need to maintain strict distance from Edward Ashcombe if she hoped to survive her position with both her reputation and her heart intact. Though even as she made this resolution, a treacherous part of her wondered if it was already too late for such precautions.

EDWARD WATCHED Charlotte's hasty departure, noting how her skirts swished around her ankles as she practically fled from his presence. The ghost of her lavender scent lingered in the air, taunting him with its delicate persistence. His fingers flexed at his sides, still tingling from that brief, accidental brush against her shoulder.

Why had she run? The question nagged at him even as he paced the length of the drawing room, his boots clicking against the polished floor. He was accustomed to women seeking his attention, not fleeing from it. Yet Miss Larkspur had all but bolted like a frightened doe, though not before he'd caught the flash of something in those remarkable hazel eyes—something that mirrored his own unsettling response to their proximity.

"Damn and blast," he muttered, running a hand through his already disheveled hair. The truth was, he'd felt an overwhelming urge to escape himself. The intensity of his reaction to her threatened to consume him whole like a tide rising too swiftly to outrun. One moment more in her presence and he might have done something remarkably stupid—like trace the curve of her cheek or discover if her lips were as soft as they appeared.

Edward stopped before the window, bracing his hands against the sill as he stared unseeing at the manicured gardens below. He'd known countless beautiful women, had dallied with more than his share of them. Yet none had affected him quite like this quiet, composed governess with her gentle voice and steady gaze.

Perhaps that was precisely why she posed such a danger. The women of his usual acquaintance wore their intentions as openly as their rouge, playing the same games of seduction and conquest that he himself had mastered. But Miss Larkspur... there was nothing artificial about her. No calculated coyness or practiced allure. Just a natural grace and an intelligence that sparked something deep within him—something he'd thought long buried beneath years of cynicism and carefully cultivated reputation.

"This will not do," he declared to the empty room, straightening his shoulders with determination. The wisest course would be to maintain his distance. Let her tend to Beatrice's education while he occupied himself elsewhere. Surely London held enough diversions to drive the memory of those expressive eyes and that lilting voice from his mind.

Edward strode to the drinks cabinet, pouring himself a generous measure of brandy. The familiar burn of the spirit did nothing to ease the tension coiling in his chest. He could still picture the way she'd pressed her palms against her skirts, as though anchoring herself against some internal storm. Had she felt it too —that inexplicable pull between them?

No. Better not to pursue that line of thinking. She was his sister's employee, for God's sake, and clearly a lady of proper breeding despite her reduced circumstances. The last thing she needed was to become entangled with a man of his reputation. He had no business entertaining thoughts of how perfectly her small frame might fit against his chest, or how those chestnut waves might feel spilling over his pillow.

Edward drained his glass, setting it down with more force than necessary. Distance. Yes, that was the solution. He would remove himself from her orbit entirely. Let Helena handle all matters concerning the governess. He could certainly find plenty of excuses to remain in London, far from the temptation that Miss Larkspur presented.

The sudden awareness that he was already planning his retreat—he, who had never backed down from any challenge or denied himself any pleasure—only served to underscore the danger she represented. When had he become a man who ran from his own desires?

But this was different. Something about Miss Larkspur bypassed all his carefully constructed defenses, threatening to upend the comfortable cynicism he'd wrapped around himself like armor. Better to withdraw now, before that penetrating gaze of hers saw too deeply into the corners of his soul he preferred to keep shadowed.

He was the Duke of Blackwood, after all, and Dukes do not play around with the help. Generations of noble ancestors would surely rise from their graves in horror at the mere thought of him dallying with a governess, no matter how bewitching her smile or how gracefully she carried herself through his halls. The very foundations of proper society would quake at such an impropriety, and he had caused enough scandals without adding this particular transgression to his notorious reputation.

A gentle knock echoed through the drawing room, pulling Edward from his brooding thoughts. Helena entered, her mourning dress rustling softly as she crossed the threshold. One glance at her brother's tense posture and distant expression told her all she needed to know—he was troubled by something.

Edward remained by the window, his fingers wrapped around the empty brandy glass as if it might anchor him to reality. The afternoon sun cast long shadows across the Persian carpet, marking the passage of time he'd spent lost in contemplation.

"I trust you've had sufficient time to form an opinion of Miss Larkspur?" Helena's voice carried its usual gentle tone, though her eyes studied her brother's profile with shrewd attention.

"Hmm?" Edward didn't turn from the window. "Oh, yes. She seems... suitable."

Helena's brow furrowed at his distracted response. In all their years together, she had learned to read the subtle nuances in her brother's manner. This abstracted air was most unlike him. "If you have reservations about her presence at Blackwood, I can—"

"No." Edward's response came too quickly, too forcefully. He cleared his throat and modulated his tone. "That won't be necessary."

"Are you certain? I can put an end to her employment immediately if you think—"

"Helena." Edward finally turned to face his sister, his expression carefully composed. "Miss Larkspur will be a good influence for Beatrice. I see no reason to dismiss her."

The corners of Helena's mouth lifted in a small, knowing smile. She had not missed the way her brother's fingers tightened around the glass at the mention of dismissing the governess, nor the careful way he avoided meeting her eyes when speaking Miss Larkspur's name.

"Well, I am pleased you approve." Helena smoothed her skirts, hiding her satisfaction. "Beatrice has taken quite a shine to her already."

"Has she?" Edward set the glass down with precise movements. "That's... fortunate."

Helena watched as her brother prowled across the room like a caged tiger, his usual grace somehow transformed into restless energy. Yes, Miss Larkspur's presence would certainly prove interesting, though perhaps not solely for Beatrice's benefit.

"Most fortunate indeed," Helena murmured, more to herself than to her brother. She recognized the signs of internal struggle in Edward's manner—the tight set of his shoulders, the way his hand repeatedly raked through his hair, the unusual quietness that had replaced his typical sharp wit.

"Though I trust you'll ensure Miss Larkspur understands her duties and the... proper boundaries of her position," Edward added, still avoiding his sister's penetrating gaze.

"Of course." Helena allowed a touch of amusement to color her tone. "I'm sure Miss Larkspur is quite aware of her place within the household."

Edward's jaw tightened almost imperceptibly at her words. "Good. That's... good."

Helena moved to the bell pull, preparing to summon tea, but paused to observe her brother once more. The afternoon light caught the tension in his face, highlighting the conflict that seemed to war beneath his carefully maintained facade. Whatever had transpired during his interview with Miss Larkspur had clearly left its mark.

"Shall I have tea brought in?" she asked, though she suspected her brother would soon make his excuses to leave.

"No, thank you." Edward straightened his cravat, which had somehow become askew during his pacing. "I believe I'll ride out for a while. Clear my head."

"Of course." Helena watched as he strode toward the door, his movements precise and controlled. "Though Edward?"

He paused at the threshold, his hand resting on the doorframe. "Yes?"

"Miss Larkspur will be joining us for dinner this evening. I believe it important to make her feel welcome as a member of our household."

The barely perceptible stiffening of his shoulders told Helena all she needed to know about her brother's state of mind. "As you wish," he replied, his voice carefully neutral before he disappeared into the corridor.

Helena allowed herself a small smile as she pulled the bell for tea. Yes, she was very pleased indeed with her choice of governess, though perhaps not entirely for the reasons she had originally anticipated.

CHAPTER FOUR
unexpected encounters

An intimate gathering of society's finest had assembled at Blackwood Estate for tea and light entertainment. The sweet perfume of fresh-cut roses mingled with the delicate aroma of Earl Grey, creating an atmosphere of refined comfort that suited the casual nature of the occasion.

In a corner near the window, Charlotte sat with young Beatrice, who had scattered her colored pencils across a small table as she drew with fierce concentration. The child's tongue poked out slightly as she worked, her dark curls falling forward despite the ribbon meant to hold them back.

"Look, Miss Charlotte! I've drawn Pepper just as she looks in the garden." Beatrice held up her drawing of the estate's beloved spaniel, the artwork showing more enthusiasm than skill.

"What lovely detail you've captured in her fur." Charlotte leaned closer, pointing to the careful lines. "And see how you've made her eyes sparkle with life."

Around them, ladies in silk gowns traded gossip over delicate china cups while gentlemen discussed politics and weather in measured tones. Charlotte felt the familiar weight of her station press upon her shoulders - not quite a servant, yet decidedly not one of them. She smoothed her modest muslin dress, aware of its simplicity among the fashionable attire surrounding her.

The drawing room's double doors swept open with dramatic flair, and the Duke of Blackwood strode in. His entrance commanded attention without effort, his tall frame cutting an impressive figure in a perfectly tailored dark blue coat. A roguish smile played at his lips as he nodded to various acquaintances.

"Your Grace, we'd nearly given up hope of seeing you today." Lady Pembroke's voice carried across the room, tinged with obvious flirtation.

"I find arriving fashionably late keeps life interesting, wouldn't you agree?" His rich baritone held a note of practiced charm that made several young ladies titter behind their fans.

Charlotte watched as he navigated the room with the ease of long practice, noting how his apparent nonchalance masked a restlessness in his bearing.

Edward moved through his guests with practiced grace, pausing before Lady Pembroke and her daughter Margaret. The latter blushed prettily as he bent to kiss her gloved hand, her golden curls bouncing as she dipped into a curtsey. "My dear Lady Pembroke, you grow lovelier each time I see you. And Miss Maribelle, that shade of pink suits you remarkably well." He delivered the compliments with a lazy smile that had won him countless hearts across London's ballrooms. Lady Pembroke preened under his attention, while Maribelle's cheeks flushed deeper, matching the silk of her gown.

Though he maintained his focus on the ladies before him, his awareness of Charlotte's presence in the corner of the room gnawed at him like a persistent ache. His eyes, rebellious things that they were, stole glances in her direction as if drawn by an invisible thread. The sight of her bent close to Beatrice, their heads together over some childish artwork, stirred something uncomfortable in his chest. She wore a simple blue muslin dress that should have rendered her invisible among the flashier silks and satins of his guests, yet he found his gaze returning to the gentle curve of her neck, the way her chestnut curls caught the afternoon light. When Lady Pembroke made some witty observation about the weather, he forced a laugh, though he had scarcely heard her words.

Edward extricated himself from Lady Pembroke's circle with the smooth efficiency of a man who had practiced such social maneuvers countless times before. His polished boots clicked against the parquet flooring as he crossed the drawing room, each step deliberate and measured. The scattered conversations around him dimmed to hushed whispers as the assembled guests tracked his progress, their eyes darting between his determined stride and its apparent destination.

Charlotte felt his approach like a gathering storm, though she kept her attention firmly fixed on Beatrice's artistic endeavors. Her fingers tightened almost imperceptibly on the pencil she held, the only outward sign of her awareness as his tall shadow fell across their small table. The space between them crackled with an energy that defied the strict social boundaries of their respective positions, and even young Beatrice paused in her drawing, looking up with wide-eyed curiosity at her uncle's sudden proximity.

Around them, the air grew thick with speculation as matrons and debutantes alike observed this unconventional interaction, their teacups forgotten in their hands. The Duke's reputation as a determined rake lent every movement he made an air of scandal, yet there was something different in his bearing now - a peculiar softness that seemed at odds with his usual rakish demeanor.

His blue eyes, typically sharp with cynicism or dancing with practiced charm, held an unfamiliar warmth as they settled on the tableau before him, and the slight tension in his jaw suggested this was no casual social call.

"Miss Larkspur. I trust my niece isn't exhausting your patience with her artistic endeavors?"

"Not at all, Your Grace. Her dedication to improvement is most admirable."

"Uncle Edward!" Beatrice bounced in her seat. "Would you like to see my drawing of Pepper?"

A genuine smile softened his features as he bent to examine the artwork. "Remarkable likeness. Though perhaps Pepper's ears are a touch smaller in reality?"

"They're exactly right," Beatrice declared with all the conviction of her five years.

Charlotte couldn't help but smile at their exchange, noticing how his presence seemed to fill the space around them, making the rest of the room fade to insignificance. The moment shattered as a melodic voice cut through their bubble.

"Your Grace! You simply must settle a debate we're having about the opera." Miss Victoria Ashworth glided forward, her cream-colored gown rustling with each step. Her golden curls bounced as she placed a delicate hand on the Duke's arm. "Lady Pembroke insists that the new soprano at Covent Garden surpasses Madame Catalani, but I cannot agree."

Edward straightened, his mask of easy charm sliding back into place. "Far be it from me to leave such an important matter unresolved." He allowed Miss Ashworth to lead him away, though Charlotte caught a fleeting look of resignation cross his features.

Charlotte returned her attention to Beatrice's drawing, ignoring the hollow feeling in her chest as Miss Ashworth's tinkling laughter floated across the room. She had no right to feel disappointed by the Duke's departure - after all, what could a mere governess expect from such a man of consequence? She picked up a colored pencil and began helping Beatrice shade Pepper's coat, focusing on the simple pleasure of making a child smile rather than the ache of wishes that could never be fulfilled.

Charlotte looked up to watch the ladies of leisure float about the drawing room like exotic butterflies, their silk gowns rustling with each graceful movement. Miss Ashworth's golden ringlets caught the afternoon light as she leaned closer to the Duke, her tinkling laugh a melody of practiced charm. How different their worlds were - these women who had nothing more pressing to consider than which color ribbon best matched their complexion or which gentleman might lead them in the next dance.

Her fingers absently smoothed the serviceable muslin of her own gown. Though clean and well-maintained, it bore little resemblance to the frothy confections that surrounded her. *If only for a day,* she thought, *to experience such freedom. To wear silk that whispered against her skin, to feel ostrich feathers tickle her cheek, to have gentlemen hang upon her every word...*

"Miss Charlotte!" Beatrice's urgent whisper broke through her musings. "Look there - through the window! The bees are dancing in the garden, just like you taught me about. May we go watch them? Please?"

Charlotte glanced at the gathering, where Lady Helena was deep in conversation with several matrons, while the Duke remained thoroughly ensnared by Miss Ashworth's charms. No one would miss a governess and her charge slipping away for a brief educational interlude.

"Very quietly now," Charlotte whispered back, gathering Beatrice's scattered art supplies. "Like mice in the pantry."

Beatrice giggled, pressing her hands to her mouth to stifle the sound. Her eyes sparkled with conspiracy as she tiptoed toward the French doors that led to the garden terrace, Charlotte following close behind.

The warm afternoon air embraced them as they stepped outside, carrying the sweet perfume of late summer roses. Beatrice skipped ahead, her dark curls bouncing with each step, while Charlotte inhaled deeply, feeling the tension in her shoulders ease. Here, among the perfectly manicured flower beds and humming insects, she need not measure every word and gesture against society's exacting standards.

"Look, Miss Charlotte! They're gathering nectar from the lavender." Beatrice dropped to her knees beside a flowering bush, her sketch paper already in hand. "Will you help me draw them?"

"Of course, my dear." Charlotte settled beside her charge, smoothing her skirts beneath her. "But remember what we discussed about observing bees?"

"Keep very still and quiet, so they don't feel threatened." Beatrice's voice dropped to a reverent whisper. "Then they'll let us watch their important work."

Charlotte's heart swelled with affection for this precious child who absorbed knowledge like a sponge, whose curiosity remained untainted by society's restrictive expectations. She helped Beatrice position her paper against a wooden drawing board, guiding her small hand as they sketched the basic shape of a bee in flight.

The garden hummed with life around them - bees dancing from flower to flower, butterflies drifting on warm currents of air, birds calling from the oak trees that lined the estate's grounds. Here, Charlotte could almost forget the weight of her position, the constant awareness of her limitations. Here, she was simply a woman sharing nature's wonders with an eager child.

"Your wings aren't quite right," Beatrice observed, studying their joint effort with a critical eye. "Bee wings are more delicate, like gossamer."

"Indeed they are." Charlotte smiled at the child's precise vocabulary. "Shall we try again?"

Charlotte knelt beside Beatrice near a patch of violets. The little girl's face lit up with delight as she inhaled their delicate fragrance.

"Miss Charlotte, look! A butterfly!" Beatrice pointed at a painted lady dancing through the air, its orange wings catching the sunlight. Before Charlotte could react, Beatrice darted after it, her dark curls bouncing as she disappeared around a hedge.

"Beatrice! Come back this instant!" Charlotte gathered her skirts and rushed after her charge, rounding the corner at full speed—only to collide with a solid form. Strong hands steadied her shoulders as she stumbled backward.

"I see you're in quite a hurry, Miss Larkspur," the Duke of Blackwood's deep voice carried a note of amusement.

Charlotte's cheeks flushed. "Your Grace! I apologize—Beatrice has run off chasing a butterfly."

Edward whipped his head around the garden. His niece was nowhere to be found. "Then we'd best find her before she ventures too far."

Charlotte hesitated for a moment before taking her place beside him. They walked together down the garden path, her skin tingling by the sheer nearness of his presence.

"I often found myself chasing butterflies at her age," the Duke mused. "Though I dare say I gave my governess far more trouble than sweet Beatrice gives you."

"I cannot imagine you as a troublesome child, Your Grace."

"No? I suppose my current reputation precedes me." He glanced sideways at her. "Do you read much, Miss Larkspur?"

"When time permits. I'm particularly fond of poetry—Wordsworth's nature verses speak to my soul."

His eyes brightened. "Indeed? I've always preferred Byron myself, though I must admit Wordsworth has a way of capturing the sublime in the simplest things."

They paused at a fork in the path, and Charlotte spotted a flash of blue muslin through the rose bushes. "There she is!"

They found Beatrice crouched beside a flowering shrub, watching the butterfly rest on a bloom. The Duke knelt beside her, his voice softening. "You've found quite a treasure, little one."

"Uncle Edward, isn't she beautiful?" Beatrice whispered, careful not to startle the creature.

"Indeed she is." He met Charlotte's gaze over Beatrice's head. "Though perhaps not the most beautiful sight in this garden."

Charlotte's heart fluttered traitorously. The Duke's expression grew distant as he watched the butterfly take wing.

"Sometimes I envy their freedom," he murmured. "To float above it all, unburdened by expectations or the weight of one's name."

"Do you find it very heavy then? Your name?"

"Heavier with each passing season. The ton has certain expectations of a duke—particularly one with my... history." His jaw tightened. "They wait for my next scandal like vultures circling carrion."

Charlotte's hand moved of its own accord to touch his arm. "Perhaps they would see differently if you allowed them to know the man who discusses poetry in gardens and delights in butterflies with his niece."

Their eyes met, and for a moment, Charlotte glimpsed something raw and vulnerable in his gaze. But before he could respond, voices carried across the garden.

> "Is that the Duke of Blackwood?"
>
> "With the governess?"
>
> "How shocking! Though I suppose we shouldn't be surprised, given his proclivities..."

The Duke straightened, his face hardening into its usual mask of aristocratic indifference. "Ladies," he called out, offering a bow that managed to be both proper and dismissive. "If you'll excuse me, I have business to attend to."

He strode away without another glance at Charlotte, leaving her to shepherd Beatrice back toward the house. Her fingers still tingled where they had touched his coat, and her mind whirled with the memory of his unguarded expression.

From her position near the garden entrance, Charlotte observed the Duke of Blackwood as he navigated through the cluster of elegant ladies who had interrupted their moment. His easy charm and graceful manners drew admiring glances and tinkling laughter from the assembled women.

Miss Ashworth touched his arm with her gloved hand, leaning close to whisper something that made him smile—that devastatingly handsome half-smile that had caused Charlotte's breath to catch mere moments ago in the garden. Now it belonged to another, as was proper.

Charlotte busied herself straightening Beatrice's sash, though her eyes kept straying to the gathering. Miss Penelope Rutledge's golden curls caught the afternoon sun as she tilted her head coquettishly, while Lady Margaret's emerald silk gown rustled with each deliberate movement closer to the Duke.

"Miss Charlotte, may we go see the kittens in the stable?" Beatrice tugged at her sleeve.

"In a moment, dear." Charlotte's attention remained fixed on the scene before her. The ladies' jewels sparkled as brightly as their wit, their refined manners a stark contrast to her own modest deportment.

Yet it was not their material advantages that caused the hollow ache in her chest. It was the simple freedom they possessed—the right to engage him in conversation without censure, to seek his attention without scandal, to hope for his regard without impossibility.

The Duke laughed at something Lady Ashworth said, the rich sound carrying across the garden. Charlotte remembered how that same laugh had softened when he spoke to Beatrice about the butterfly, how his eyes had held a different light entirely when discussing poetry with her.

But she was the governess. Her position demanded discretion, restraint, and above all, distance. The garden wall at her back felt less confining than the invisible barriers of propriety that separated her from that glittering group.

"Your company seems far more preferable to theirs," a voice murmured near her ear.

Charlotte started. Lady Helena had appeared beside her, watching the same scene with knowing eyes.

"My lady, I was just—"

"Observing my brother's admirers? Yes, they do tend to flock around him like peacocks in a garden." Helena's tone held a touch of sisterly exasperation. "Though I daresay none of them have ever discussed Wordsworth with him."

Charlotte's cheeks burned. "You heard?"

"I hear a great many things, Miss Larkspur. Including the genuine interest in Edward's voice when he speaks with you." Helena's gaze hardened, her blue eyes taking on the same steely quality that her brother's often possessed when confronted with an uncomfortable truth. Her fingers absently traced the delicate lace trim of her sleeve as she continued, "But take care, Miss Larkspur, do not get entangled in my brother's web. Though I care for you deeply, my first duty must be to Beatrice and this household's reputation. If you are ruined, you are also banished from this house. There can be no exceptions, even for one as cherished as yourself."

Before Charlotte could respond, Beatrice tugged her sleeve again. "The kittens, Miss Charlotte! You promised!"

"So I did." Charlotte gathered her composure and took Beatrice's small hand. As they walked toward the stables, she allowed herself one final glance over her shoulder.

Lady Helena walked towards her brother's locale, while the Duke stood apart from his admirers now, his eyes meeting hers across the garden. For a heartbeat, that unguarded expression returned —a flash of longing that matched her own. Then Lady Ashworth reclaimed his attention, and the moment shattered like spun glass.

Charlotte turned away, her throat tight with unspoken words. She would carry out her duties, tend to Beatrice, maintain her distance. It was, after all, what was expected of a governess.

But oh, how the restrictions chafed at her heart.

CHAPTER FIVE
a moment of weakness

The evening sun cast long shadows across Blackwood Estate's manicured lawns, painting the tranquil lake in shades of amber and gold. A gentle breeze rustled through the willow trees that lined the water's edge, their graceful branches swaying in a hypnotic dance against the darkening sky.

Charlotte stood at the water's edge, her fingers absently tracing patterns on the rough bark of an ancient oak tree. The peaceful setting provided a stark contrast to the whirlwind of emotions that had plagued her thoughts since her earlier encounters with the Duke of Blackwood. Her hazel eyes reflected the shimmer of the lake as she gazed across its surface, lost in contemplation.

The weight of her position as governess pressed heavily upon her shoulders. While she took great pride in nurturing young Beatrice's education and development, the strict boundaries of propriety left little room for the dreams that had begun to take root in her heart. A sigh escaped her lips as she remembered the intensity of the Duke's gaze during their chance meeting in the garden.

Charlotte's fingers traced idle patterns in the folds of her modest gray dress as memories of the Duke's piercing blue eyes invaded her thoughts. How many times had she heard whispered tales of governesses who lost their positions—and their dignity—after falling prey to flights of romantic fancy? She had always dismissed such stories as cautionary tales meant to keep young ladies in their proper place.

"How foolish they were," she whispered to herself, her words carried away by the evening breeze. "And how much more foolish am I?"

The lake's surface rippled, disturbing her reflection. Like the water, her emotions refused to settle into the calm, controlled state she had always maintained. Her heart quickened at the mere thought of him—the way his voice softened when he spoke of his childhood, how his fingers had briefly brushed against hers as they searched for Beatrice in the garden.

"This cannot be love," Charlotte murmured, pressing her hand to her chest as if to quiet the betraying organ within. "I hardly know what love is, beyond what I've read in novels." She had never experienced the grand passion described in those pages, had never felt her breath catch at the sight of a gentleman—until now.

The memory of his rakish smile sent warmth flooding through her chest, followed swiftly by an icy dread. The Duke's reputation preceded him like a herald announcing his arrival. *How many hearts had he already broken? How many women had believed themselves special, only to be cast aside when he tired of their company?*

"I am nothing more than a passing amusement," she said firmly, though her voice wavered. "A novel distraction from his usual conquests."

The setting sun painted the clouds in shades of rose and gold, reminding her of the opulent ballrooms where ladies of quality danced and flirted behind their fans. Women who moved in his circle, who understood the rules of the ton, who could match him in wealth and status. Women who were everything Charlotte was not.

She plucked a fallen leaf from the water's edge, watching as it spun in her fingers. "The Duke will marry someone worthy of his station. Someone who can navigate his world with grace and understanding." The leaf slipped from her grasp, carried away by the current. "Not someone who must earn her bread teaching children their letters."

Her throat tightened as she imagined him dancing with some nameless beauty at his next ball, bestowing that magnetic smile on another woman. The thought shouldn't pain her so—she had no claim on his affections, no right to feel this hollow ache in her chest.

Charlotte wrapped her arms around herself, suddenly chilled despite the warm evening air. The garden's beauty seemed to mock her now, its perfectly maintained paths and elegant topiaries serving as reminders of the vast gulf between their stations. Even the flowers appeared to turn away from her presence, closing their petals as the day faded into dusk.

"I am a fool," she whispered, her voice thick with unshed tears. "A complete and utter fool to let my heart wander where it has no business going."

The distant sound of laughter drifted from the house, reminding her that she should return to her duties. Beatrice would need assistance preparing for bed soon, and Charlotte could not neglect her responsibilities simply because her heart had decided to play traitor.

She smoothed her skirts and straightened her spine, attempting to restore her usual composed demeanor. Yet beneath this carefully maintained facade, her heart continued its treacherous dance, spinning dreams of impossible futures and forbidden love.

Charlotte took one last look at the darkening twilight reflected in the lake. The water provided no answers and offered no solution to the chaos inside her. It simply kept flowing, just as society would follow its set path, taking her and the Duke in very different directions.

AT THE OTHER end of the grounds, Edward emerged from the manor house. His usually pristine cravat hung loose around his neck, and his dark hair showed signs of repeated encounters with frustrated fingers. The day's succession of tedious social obligations and whispered gossip had left him craving solitude.

Edward stalked across the manicured lawn, his boots crushing the perfectly trimmed grass beneath. The setting sun cast long shadows across the grounds, matching his dark mood. Throughout the endless parade of simpering debutantes and calculating mamas at today's garden party, his gaze had constantly searched for one particular face—a face that had been conspicuously absent.

"Damn and blast," he muttered, tugging at his cravat until it came completely undone. The silk hung limply around his neck as he continued his restless prowl of the grounds.

Lady Winchester had practically thrown her daughter in his path, and the honorable Miss Penelope had batted her eyes and giggled at his every word. In years past, he might have found such obvious pursuit amusing, perhaps even entertaining. Now it left him cold.

He paused at the edge of the lake, watching the water lap against the shore. The emptiness in his chest had grown throughout the day, an unfamiliar ache that seemed to intensify with each hour that passed without seeing Charlotte's gentle smile or hearing her quick wit.

"This is madness," he growled, running both hands through his already disheveled hair. "Complete and utter madness."

Love was a fool's game, a weakness he had sworn never to indulge. He had watched it destroy his father after his mother's death, had seen it reduce the once-proud Duke to a shell of himself. Edward had vowed then never to let himself be so vulnerable, to never give another soul such power over him.

Instead, he had lived as he pleased, taking his pleasure where he found it, caring nothing for the whispers and scandals that followed in his wake. But now...

"Thirty years old," he said to no one in particular, "and what do I have to show for it? A string of conquests and a reputation that would make even the most hardened rake blush."

The weight of his title pressed down upon him like a physical burden. The Dukedom of Blackwood had passed unbroken through fifteen generations, each Duke producing an heir to carry on the line. Now that responsibility rested solely upon his shoulders.

His thoughts turned unbidden to Charlotte with a child in her arms—*his child*. The image sent an unexpected surge of warmth through his chest, followed immediately by cold reality. She was a governess, far below his station. The ton would *never* accept such a match.

"As if she would have me anyway," he scoffed, kicking a stone into the water. "She's too intelligent not to see through my reputation."

Yet he could not shake the memory of their shared moment in the garden, the way her eyes had sparkled with humor and understanding as they discussed their mutual love of Shakespeare. No other woman had ever challenged his opinions so deftly or seen past his carefully cultivated facade with such ease.

The breeze carried the sound of distant laughter from the house, reminding him of his duties as host. No doubt the remaining guests expected him to return and play his part—the rakish Duke, the unattainable prize, the man who cared for nothing and no one.

"I could have any woman in that room," he mused, staring at his reflection in the darkening water. "Any one of them would jump at the chance to become a Duchess." The thought brought no satisfaction, only a deeper sense of that strange emptiness that had taken root in his chest.

His reflection offered no answers, only the truth he had been avoiding: somewhere between their first meeting and now, Charlotte Larkspur had managed to do what no other woman had accomplished. She had breached the walls around his heart, and he had no idea how to proceed.

Edward continued his solitary walk around the lake's perimeter, pausing occasionally to select smooth stones from the shore. With practiced motions, he sent them skipping across the water's surface, each splash echoing his turbulent thoughts. The dying sunlight caught the ripples, creating expanding circles of gold that dissolved into the darkening water.

"Seven skips," he muttered, counting the stone's bounces before it sank beneath the surface. "Better than yesterday, at least."

Movement across the lake caught his eye, and his heart performed an unwelcome somersault in his chest. Charlotte's slender figure appeared through the gathering twilight, her chestnut hair catching the last rays of sunlight. She walked with her usual quiet grace, seemingly lost in thought as she traced her fingers along the rough bark of the trees she passed.

Edward's feet moved of their own accord, taking two steps in her direction before he forced himself to halt. His fingers clenched around another stone, its edges biting into his palm. The pain provided a welcome distraction from the magnetic pull he felt toward her.

"This is precisely why you need to maintain your distance," he chided himself, forcing his gaze away from her figure. "Nothing good can come of these... feelings."

The word itself left a bitter taste in his mouth. Feelings were dangerous things, liable to lead a man astray from his proper path. Yet here he stood, like some moonstruck youth, watching a woman walk alone by the lake.

"Perhaps Lady Elizabeth might provide suitable entertainment," he mused, tossing another stone with more force than necessary. It sank immediately, creating an angry splash. "No, too vapid by half. And her mother would have the banns read before the evening was out."

Miss Maribelle crossed his mind next, with her striking beauty and sharp wit. But the thought of pursuing her brought no spark of interest, no thrill of anticipation. Instead, his treacherous eyes kept straying back to Charlotte's solitary figure across the water.

"Miss Ashworth, then?" He considered Victoria Ashworth's golden beauty and calculated charm. She would make a suitable duchess, certainly. The ton would approve of such a match. Yet the idea left him cold, empty.

Edward ran a hand through his already disheveled hair, his frustration mounting with each passing moment. "What I need is a drink. Several drinks, in fact." The thought of his well-stocked wine cellar held more appeal than any of the eligible ladies who had paraded before him that afternoon.

Across the lake, Charlotte paused in her walk, turning slightly toward the water. Even at this distance, the grace of her movement caught his attention, the simple elegance of her form more appealing than all the practiced poses of society's finest.

"Damn and blast," he swore softly, dropping the remaining stones from his hand. They clattered against each other as they fell, the sound sharp in the evening quiet. "This is precisely why I need that drink."

His neckcloth felt suddenly too tight, despite hanging loose and untied around his neck. The evening air, still warm from the day's sun, seemed to press against him with uncomfortable weight. Every fiber of his being urged him to cross the distance between them, to hear her voice, to see her eyes light up with that particular sparkle she got when preparing to challenge one of his opinions.

Instead, he forced his feet to turn toward the house, away from the temptation Charlotte presented. Each step felt heavier than the last, as though his boots had turned to lead. The sound of gravel crunching beneath his feet provided a steady rhythm to accompany his dark thoughts.

"Brandy," he decided, his stride lengthening as he approached the house. "A large glass of brandy, and perhaps this madness will subside."

But even as he reached the terrace steps, he knew no amount of spirits would erase the image of Charlotte walking alone by the lake, touched by the golden light of sunset. It would haunt his dreams tonight, as she had every night since their first meeting.

Edward paused at the top of the steps, allowing himself one final glance across the water. Charlotte had moved on, disappearing among the trees like some ethereal spirit. The lake's surface had settled, showing no evidence of his earlier stone-throwing disruption. Only the hollow ache in his chest remained as proof that she had been there at all.

CHAPTER SIX
the butterfly

The chandeliers cast their golden glow across Blackwood Estate's dining room, their light dancing off the crystal glasses and fine china that adorned the mahogany table. Lady Helena sat at one end, her posture perfect but her fingers fidgeting with her napkin as she observed the gathering before her. The evening air hung heavy with the aroma of roasted pheasant and freshly baked bread, yet beneath it all lay an undercurrent of unspoken tension.

"And then the butterfly landed right on my nose!" Beatrice's clear voice rang out above the gentle clink of silverware. She stood beside her chair, arms spread wide as she regaled her captive audience with tales of her garden adventures.

Lady Ashworth clutched her chest, her jewels glinting. "How perfectly delightful, dear child!"

"Indeed, you must tell us more about these garden escapades," Lord Pembroke encouraged, his weathered face creasing with genuine amusement.

Charlotte sat rigid in her chair, desperately focusing on cutting her meat into precise, even pieces. The weight of Edward's presence across the table pressed upon her like a physical force. She could feel the heat of his gaze, though she refused to meet it.

"Miss Larkspur," Lady Ashworth called, drawing Charlotte's attention. "You must share your secret for keeping such a spirited child so well-behaved."

"Oh, Beatrice requires little guidance in matters of charm," Charlotte replied, her voice steady despite the tremor in her hands. "She comes by it naturally."

Edward's low chuckle floated across the table, and Charlotte's knife slipped against her plate with a harsh screech. Several heads turned, but she kept her eyes fixed downward.

At the far end of the table, Edward found himself trapped in conversation with Miss Penelope Winchester, who simpered and batted her eyelashes with practiced precision. His responses came automatically, years of social training taking over while his thoughts drifted to stolen moments in the garden, to hazel eyes that held more wisdom than all the social butterflies in London combined.

"Don't you agree, Your Grace?" Miss Winchester's voice pierced through his reverie.

"Entirely," he replied smoothly, though he hadn't heard a word she'd said. His gaze slid involuntarily toward Charlotte, catching her in a rare unguarded moment as she smiled tenderly at Beatrice.

Lady Helena watched this delicate dance with growing concern, noting how her brother's customary charm seemed hollow tonight, how his attention kept straying across the table. She observed Charlotte's careful composure, the way the young governess seemed to hold herself together through sheer force of will.

"More wine, Your Grace?" A footman appeared at Edward's elbow.

"Yes," he answered perhaps too quickly, earning a sharp look from his sister.

Beatrice, oblivious to the undercurrents swirling around her, launched into another tale. "And then Miss Larkspur showed me how to make daisy chains! Uncle Edward, remember when you helped us gather the flowers?"

Charlotte's cheeks flushed pink at the memory, and she busied herself with her wine glass. The moment felt suspended in amber – Beatrice's innocent reminder hanging in the air, Edward's presence across the table growing more acute with each passing second, the weight of propriety and position pressing down upon them all.

Lady Helena cleared her throat softly. "Beatrice, darling, perhaps we should let our guests enjoy their dinner. You can share more stories during dessert."

Charlotte pushed her pheasant around her plate, the delicate flavors now tasting like ash in her mouth. The crystal chandelier's light caught in the amber depths of her wine, and she found herself mesmerized by its depths, seeking refuge from the chaos of her thoughts.

"I find the season particularly delightful this year," Miss Ashworth's voice carried across the table, sweet as honey and just as cloying. "Though perhaps not as exciting as previous ones. Wouldn't you say, Your Grace?"

Charlotte's fork scraped against fine china as her hand trembled. Every laugh, every clink of silverware, every rustle of silk seemed to mock her predicament. *How foolish she'd been in the garden, allowing herself to believe, even for a moment, that there could be something more. A governess and a duke? The very notion bordered on absurd.*

Yet the memory of Edward's fingers brushing against hers as they'd gathered daisies with Beatrice refused to fade. The way his eyes had softened when he spoke of his childhood, the vulnerable crack in his voice when he'd confessed his weariness of society's expectations - these moments had carved themselves into her heart with treacherous permanence.

"Miss Larkspur?" Lady Helena's gentle inquiry startled her from her reverie. "Are you quite well? You've barely touched your food."

"Perfectly well, my lady," Charlotte managed, forcing a smile that felt brittle on her lips. "Perhaps just a touch warm."

The lie felt leaden on her tongue. In truth, her skin prickled with awareness of Edward's presence, even as she steadfastly avoided looking in his direction. The sound of his deep laugh at something Miss Ashworth said sent an unwelcome shiver down her spine.

Beatrice tugged at Charlotte's sleeve. "Miss Larkspur, may I tell everyone about the bird's nest we found?"

"Of course, dear," Charlotte replied, grateful for the distraction. She smoothed Beatrice's dark curls, finding comfort in this simple, permissible gesture of affection.

Charlotte's resolve weakened for just a moment, and her eyes flicked upward, seeking him out despite her better judgment. Her breath caught as she found Edward's intense gaze already fixed upon her, his blue eyes dark with an emotion she dared not name. The connection lasted barely a heartbeat before she tore her gaze away, heat flooding her cheeks.

Foolish, foolish woman, she chastised herself, gripping her wine glass too tightly. *What did she expect? That he would declare himself before all of society?* That Miss Ashworth and Miss Winchester would simply step aside and allow a mere governess to capture one of the most eligible dukes in England?

"More wine, miss?" A footman appeared at her elbow.

"No, thank you," Charlotte whispered, though in truth, she desperately wished for something stronger to dull the ache in her chest. She forced herself to focus on Beatrice's animated chatter, on Lady Helena's gentle responses, on anything but the man whose presence dominated the room like a gathering storm.

"Your Grace," Miss Winchester's voice cut through Charlotte's thoughts once more, "you simply must tell us about your plans for the upcoming ball. I hear it's to be quite the spectacular affair."

Charlotte's heart constricted at the reminder. *The ball* - where Edward would be expected to dance with every eligible young lady in attendance, where she would be relegated to the shadows, watching from a distance as society played out its elaborate courtship rituals. Where every smile, every touch of his hand on another woman's waist would be a reminder of the insurmountable distance between their worlds.

THE EVENING DREW to a close with the gentle clink of silverware and the murmur of polite farewells. Charlotte's fingers trembled as she folded her napkin, her peripheral vision catching Edward's movements across the table. The weight of unspoken words pressed heavily upon the dining room, making even the simplest gesture feel laden with meaning.

"Come along, Miss Beatrice. Time for your bedtime story." Charlotte's voice carried a forced brightness as she rose from her chair. The young girl bounded toward her with eager steps, her earlier exuberance somewhat dimmed by the lateness of the hour.

"But I'm not tired at all," Beatrice protested through a poorly concealed yawn, her small hand slipping into Charlotte's.

Lady Helena watched the exchange with maternal fondness, though her eyes darted between her brother and the governess with growing concern. Edward stood near the fireplace, his tall frame casting long shadows across the Persian carpet, his attention fixed upon Charlotte's retreating form with an intensity that spoke volumes.

The guests filtered out of the dining room in small groups, their chatter echoing through the corridors of Blackwood Estate. Each click of their heels against the marble floor seemed to heighten the tension that lingered in their wake.

Edward's fingers drummed against the mantelpiece, his knuckles white with tension as he watched Charlotte disappear up the grand staircase with Beatrice. The candlelight caught the sharp angles of his face, highlighting the muscle that twitched in his jaw.

"I say, Blackwood, you seem rather distracted this evening." Lord Pembroke's voice grated against Edward's already frayed nerves.

"Not at all." Edward turned, forcing his features into a mask of casual indifference. "Simply contemplating the brandy selection for our next gathering." The lie slipped easily from his lips, though his thoughts remained fixed on the gentle sway of Charlotte's skirts as she'd ascended the stairs.

Lady Rutherford tittered behind her fan. "Do ensure you select something exceptional. Though I dare say your current offering is divine."

"Your praise is too kind," Edward replied, the words tasting like ash in his mouth. His gaze drifted once more to the empty doorway, and he cursed himself for his weakness.

Helena observed her brother's restlessness with growing unease. She excused herself from a conversation with the Countess of Marlowe and crossed the room with purposeful steps. "Edward, might I have a word?" Her tone brooked no argument as she gestured toward the adjacent drawing room.

The siblings stepped away from the gathering, the heavy door closing behind them with a soft click. Helena's silk skirts rustled as she turned to face her brother, concern etched across her delicate features.

"Your behavior this evening has been most peculiar." Helena's voice dropped to a whisper. "The way you watch Miss Larkspur—it has not gone unnoticed."

Edward's spine stiffened. "I haven't the faintest idea what you mean."

"Do not play the fool with me, brother. I saw how you could barely tear your eyes from her during dinner." Helena's words carried the weight of sisterly devotion tinged with worry. "Whatever your intentions might be—"

"My intentions?" Edward's laugh held no humor. "You presume too much, dear sister. I have no intentions whatsoever regarding Miss Larkspur or any other woman in this household."

"Edward—"

"Enough!" His voice cracked like a whip in the quiet room. "I will not stand here and be lectured about propriety by my younger sister." Hot anger coursed through his veins, fueled by the truth in Helena's observations and his own inability to master his feelings.

"I speak only out of concern—"

"Your concern is neither required nor welcomed." Edward's words cut through the air between them. He spun on his heel, his coat swirling around him as he strode toward the door.

"Where are you going?" Helena called after him.

"To get some air," he growled, yanking open the door with such force that it rattled in its frame.

The assembled guests fell silent as Edward stormed through the dining room, their conversations dying mid-sentence. Lady Rutherford's fan stopped its constant motion, and Lord Pembroke's brandy glass froze halfway to his lips.

"Your Grace?" someone ventured, but Edward paid them no heed.

He swept past them all, his boots echoing against the floor as he made his way toward the entrance hall. The weight of their stares pressed against his back, their whispers already beginning to rise in his wake. *Let them talk,* he thought bitterly. *They would do so regardless.*

The cool evening air hit his face as he emerged onto the terrace, but it did nothing to calm the storm raging within him. His hands clenched into fists at his sides as he tried to banish the image of Charlotte's face from his mind—the way her eyes had sparkled when Beatrice had made her laugh, the subtle flush that had colored her cheeks whenever their gazes had met across the table.

Behind him, the sounds of the gathering continued to drift through the windows, a reminder of the life he was expected to lead, the duties he was bound to fulfill.

Edward exited the balcony into an empty room, his restlessness manifested in the way he paced the length of it, his fingers drumming against his thigh in an erratic rhythm. The emptiness of the house pressed in around him, broken only by distant laughter and the soft rustle of servants clearing away the evening's debris.

This ends now...

His feet carried him through the familiar corridors of his ancestral home, past portraits of stern-faced ancestors and elaborate tapestries that had witnessed generations of Blackwood secrets. The soft glow of wall sconces cast dancing shadows that seemed to mock his inner turmoil.

IN A SECLUDED ALCOVE, tucked away from prying eyes, Charlotte stood with her back pressed against the cool stone wall. Her chest rose and fell with rapid breaths as she attempted to collect her scattered thoughts. The darkness wrapped around her like a protective cloak, offering temporary sanctuary from the tempest of emotions that threatened to overwhelm her.

The sound of approaching footsteps sent her heart racing. She recognized the cadence of his walk, the confident stride that could belong to none other than Edward. His presence filled the small space before he even appeared, the air growing thick with anticipation.

"Miss Larkspur," Edward's voice cut through the darkness, rich and smooth as aged brandy. He moved closer, the dim light catching the sharp angles of his face. "It seems even the most captivating company could not hold my attention."

Charlotte's breath caught in her throat as she met his intense gaze. "You should be more careful in your pursuits, Your Grace," she returned, her voice carrying a playful lilt despite the warning in her words.

The space between them crackled with electricity, each heartbeat drawing them inexorably closer. "Perhaps it's not pursuit I need," Edward murmured, his voice dropping to a whisper that sent shivers down her spine. "But to distinguish this fire."

His fingers found hers in the darkness, the touch igniting sparks beneath her skin. Charlotte's defenses crumbled as he drew her closer, the heat of his body calling to her like a siren's song.

Acting on a surge of audacious impulse, Charlotte closed the distance between them, capturing Edward's lips with her own. The kiss scorched them both with the intensity of illicit longing, conveying the weight of countless lingering gazes and unspoken words. As their mouths melded together, Edward's arms encircled her waist, pulling her tighter against him. The world around them faded into obscurity, leaving only the exquisite sensation of this moment, this connection.

Edward's tongue traced the seam of Charlotte's lips, seeking entrance, and she parted them willingly, inviting him in. Their tongues danced together, hungrily exploring the uncharted territory of their shared desire. Charlotte's hands found their way to Edward's chest, her fingers splaying across the hard planes of his muscles as she clung to him, seeking anchorage in the swirling maelstrom of passion.

Edward's hands slid down the curve of Charlotte's hips, eliciting a gasp from her as he pulled her even closer, the evidence of his arousal pressing insistently against her. She could feel the rapid thud of his heartbeat, matching the frantic rhythm of her own. The heat emanating from their entwined bodies threatened to consume them both, and Charlotte surrendered herself to the inferno of their desire.

Edward's mouth blazed a trail down Charlotte's neck, grazing her sensitive flesh with his teeth while suckling fervently. Arching her back, Charlotte granted him further access, shuddering as pleasure swelled within her. His nimble fingers unfastened her gown, revealing the milky smoothness of her shoulder. Edward's lips eagerly pursued the freshly exposed skin, igniting it with a scorching path of kisses.

Edward pressed Charlotte firmly against the wall, his hands deftly hiking her skirts to her waist. With an urgency that mirrored his own, she lifted one leg, allowing him greater access. He seized the opportunity, tugging her stockings down to her ankles, baring her smooth, creamy thighs. The friction of their bodies, now unencumbered by fabric, sent a jolt of electricity through them both, intensifying their shared desire.

Edward continued to kiss Charlotte with an intensity that left her breathless. His lips moved hungrily over hers, his tongue darting in and out of her mouth as he explored every crevice. The passion in his kisses was matched only by the heat that radiated from his body as he held her up against the wall.

As their lips parted, Edward's gaze locked onto Charlotte's eyes, his own filled with raw desire. Without breaking eye contact, he began to pull down her shift, revealing the delicate beauty of her breasts. His fingers traced the outline of each perfect mound before he lowered his head and took one into his mouth.

Charlotte moaned softly as Edward's tongue swirled around her nipple, sending shivers down her spine. She clung to his shoulders, arching her back as he paid homage to her body with reverence and passion. The sensation was unlike anything she had ever experienced before – it was as if every nerve ending in her body was on fire.

As Edward continued to worship Charlotte's breasts, she felt a sudden urgency building within her. She wanted him – needed him – more than anything in the world. With a desperate cry, she pushed herself away from the wall and pulled him towards the floor below them. They landed with a soft thud, their bodies entwined in a passionate embrace.

Without hesitation, Charlotte reached down and fumbled with Edward's trousers until she had freed his erection from its confines. She ran her fingers along its length before wrapping them around it tightly and guiding it towards her entrance. Edward groaned deeply as she positioned herself over him and slowly sank down onto his shaft, taking him inside her completely.

The sensation was overwhelming—her virgin pain subsiding—every inch of Edward filled her completely and sent waves of pleasure coursing through her body. She leaned forward, pressing herself against him as they began to move together in perfect harmony. Their bodies slid against each other with an ease that spoke volumes about their connection – it was as if they were made for each other in every possible way.

As they continued to move together, their passion grew more intense by the second. Charlotte could feel Edward's heart pounding against hers as they thrust into each other with an urgency that bordered on madness. The walls around them seemed to fade away entirely as they lost themselves in this primal dance of desire – nothing else mattered but the two of them and the intense pleasure they were sharing together at this moment in time.

Finally, after what felt like an eternity of blissful ecstasy, Charlotte could feel herself approaching climax. With a cry of pure pleasure, she threw herself forward onto Edward's chest and clung to him tightly as wave after wave of orgasmic bliss washed over her like a tidal wave crashing against the shoreline...

CHAPTER SEVEN
whispers of scandal

Days passed at Blackwood Estate, yet the memory of their copulation clung to Charlotte like a whisper in the wind. She resolved to bury her feelings beneath layers of responsibility, immersing herself in the education of young Beatrice, whose bright eyes brimmed with curiosity. Today, the lesson at hand was Greek history, the tales of gods and heroes capturing Beatrice's imagination in the sun-drenched drawing room.

The afternoon sunlight streamed through the tall windows of the drawing room, casting a golden glow upon the scattered papers and illustrated texts spread across the mahogany table. Charlotte sat beside Beatrice, who bounced eagerly in her chair as they pored over drawings of ancient Greek deities.

"And Zeus lived on Mount Olympus?" Beatrice's small finger traced the outline of a mountain peak rendered in faded ink. "With all the other gods?"

"Indeed." Charlotte adjusted the ribbon in Beatrice's dark curls that had come loose during her animated studying. "He ruled over the heavens and earth from his throne high above the mortal world."

"But why did he turn into animals to chase ladies? That seems rather silly for a king of gods." Beatrice's nose wrinkled. "Especially a swan. Swans are mean."

Charlotte felt heat rise to her cheeks. Trust a child to zero in on the more scandalous aspects of mythology that she had attempted to gloss over. "Perhaps we should focus on Athena instead. She was the goddess of wisdom and—"

"Did she ever turn into animals?" Beatrice interrupted, her blue eyes sparkling with mischief.

"No, she was known for her intelligence and skill in battle." Charlotte flipped through the pages, searching for a more appropriate illustration. "She helped many heroes on their quests."

"Like Perseus?" Beatrice bounced higher, nearly knocking over the inkwell. "With the snake-lady's head?"

"Medusa," Charlotte corrected gently, steadying the ink. "And yes, Athena guided Perseus in his quest to defeat the Gorgon."

"Why did Medusa have snakes for hair? Did she not brush it properly? Nurse always says if I don't brush my hair it will become a rat's nest, but snakes seem much worse than rats."

The rapid-fire questions made Charlotte's head spin. She pressed her fingers to her temple, where a dull ache had begun to form. "It was a punishment from Athena, though perhaps we should save that particular story for when you're older."

"But why?" Beatrice tilted her head, dark curls falling across her face. "Was she naughty? Did she not eat her vegetables? Cook says I'll turn green if I don't eat my peas, but I think having snake hair would be much more interesting than being green."

"I assure you, neither will happen if you skip your vegetables, though I still encourage you to eat them." Charlotte reached for her cup of tea, now gone cold, hoping the liquid might fortify her against the barrage of inquiries.

"What about Hercules? Did he have to eat vegetables to become strong?" Beatrice grabbed another book, nearly upending the entire stack. "Or was it because his father was Zeus? Can gods' children skip their vegetables?"

"I believe Hercules earned his strength through completing his twelve labors," Charlotte managed, catching the toppling books. "Though I'm certain a proper diet didn't hurt."

"Twelve! That's ever so many. I can barely complete my one labor of sitting still for lessons." Beatrice giggled, proving her point by sliding halfway off her chair. "Did he have to clean the stables? I heard Thomas complaining about cleaning the stables yesterday. He said it was a Herculean task!" Her face lit up with recognition. "Is that why they say that? Because Hercules had to clean stables too?"

Charlotte's head throbbed harder as she tried to keep pace with Beatrice's lightning-quick mental leaps. "Yes, the Augean stables was one of his labors. He had to clean them in a single day."

"How did he do it? Did he have a very big broom? Or did Zeus help with a lightning bolt?" Beatrice mimed sweeping with elaborate gestures. "Though I suppose lightning would just make everything catch fire, and then he'd be in even more trouble. I got in trouble last week for tracking mud into the hall, but at least it wasn't stable muck. Do you think Hercules got sent to bed without supper for making a mess?"

The room seemed to tilt slightly as Charlotte attempted to follow the dizzying path of Beatrice's logic. She reached again for her tea, only to remember it was empty. "He actually diverted two rivers to wash the stables clean."

"Rivers! That's much cleverer than a broom. Though I suppose the horses got quite wet. Did they catch colds? When I fell in the pond last spring, I was abed for three days with sniffles. Do immortal horses get sniffles?"

Just as Charlotte elaborated on the exploits of *sniffles*, a gentle knock on the door interrupted their session. A maid appeared her expression discreet yet knowing, as she approached Charlotte with a folded note clutched in her hand.

"From His Grace," the maid said, her voice barely above a whisper, as if the very mention of the Duke could ignite scandal.

Charlotte's heart raced. She accepted the note, feeling the weight of Edward's intention pressed into the edges of the parchment. With Beatrice engrossed in a colorful drawing of Mount Olympus, Charlotte carefully opened the note, her breath hitching at the elegant script that flowed across the page.

Dearest Charlotte,

Join me at the secluded lakeside cabin when the clock strikes midnight. This ardent flame refuses to be extinguished. I yearn to bask in your intoxicating presence once more.

Yours, Edward

Charlotte's heart thudded painfully in her chest. The words danced before her, taunting her moral compass and her sense of duty. A wave of battered emotion crashed over her—excitement, longing, but also a fierce sense of propriety that tangled with her desires.

"No," she murmured softly, shaking her head as if denying the invitation itself. She took a deep breath and closed her eyes, recalling their kisses and the potent attraction that had ignited in the shadows.

I cannot.

At once, Charlotte felt the weight of her responsibility pulling her back to the surface. If she continued to indulge in such reckless abandon, what would be the fate of her role at Blackwood? What would happen to Beatrice if she pursued this perilous attraction?

She summoned the maid, her hands trembling as she considered what must be done. "Please, deliver my response to the Duke. It is a matter of great importance."

The maid nodded, and as she left the room, Charlotte's resolve hardened against the fear that enveloped her. As she rejoined Beatrice in the lesson, her heart felt heavy with the conviction that she must refuse Edward's call—no matter how deep her feelings ran.

LATER THAT EVENING, as twilight descended, a storm brewed for Edward. The anticipation of the midnight rendezvous coursed through him, only to be extinguished abruptly. When he received the maid's message bearing Charlotte's refusal, the cold chill of despair gripped him.

"She declined,"—the words burned in his mind. The fire he felt for her rekindled fury and frustration, and in that moment, he was a tempest in a bottle. Charlotte's absence felt like a snare tightening around him, a harsh reminder of the societal cage that kept him bound.

He paced through the estate, the distance that had felt so close now stretched infinitely. Resolved to distance himself from Charlotte, he sought her out, desperate to extinguish the flames of passion that still flickered within him.

Edward stalked through the darkened corridors of Blackwood Estate, his footsteps echoing against the marble floors like thunder. His jaw clenched tight enough to crack teeth, hands balled into white-knuckled fists at his sides. The rejection burned through his veins like poison, feeding a storm of wounded pride and thwarted desire.

He knew the path to Charlotte's quarters by heart, though he'd never dared venture there before. The family wing lay quiet, with Helena occupied putting Beatrice to bed in the nursery down the hall. Perfect timing for a confrontation without interruption.

At last, he found her door—plain wood, unlike the ornate entries to the family chambers. Without ceremony, he threw it open and stepped inside, slamming it shut behind him with enough force to rattle the walls.

Charlotte jumped up from her writing desk, nearly spilling ink across the letter she'd been composing. "Your Grace! This is highly improper—"

"Improper?" Edward's laugh held no warmth. "You dare lecture me on propriety after your insulting rejection?" He advanced on her, forcing her to retreat until her back pressed against the wall. "Who do you think you are to deny me?"

Charlotte lifted her chin, meeting Edward's burning gaze despite her racing heart. "I am your sister's governess, and you are the

Duke of Blackwood. That is who we are, and that is all we can ever be."

Edward braced his hands against the wall on either side of her head, caging her with his body. The scent of her—lavender and sunshine—tormented him. "Are we nothing more than our titles?"

"What else would you have us be?" Charlotte's voice trembled with suppressed emotion. "Your reputation precedes you, Your Grace. I've heard the whispers—seen the scandalized looks. How many other women have you pursued with such fervor, only to cast them aside?"

Edward's jaw clenched. "You think me so callous? That I would treat you as just another conquest?"

"I think you're accustomed to getting whatever you desire." Charlotte pressed her palms flat against the wall behind her, resisting the urge to touch him. "But I am not a plaything for your amusement. I have worked too hard to build a respectable life here."

"Respectable?" He spat the word like a curse. "You hide behind respectability while denying what burns between us. Tell me you felt nothing when I kissed you. Tell me your heart doesn't race when I am near."

"What I feel matters not." Charlotte's eyes flashed with anger and unshed tears. "You storm in here, demanding explanations as if you own me. But you don't. I am not one of your thoroughbreds to be broken and bridled to your will."

Edward recoiled as if struck. "Is that truly what you think of me? That I wish to break you?"

"I think you're a man unused to hearing the word 'no.'" Charlotte's voice grew stronger. "You speak of passion and desire, but what of tomorrow? What of the day after? When society discovers that the Duke has bedded his sister's governess, who do you think will bear the greater shame?"

"I would never allow—"

"You cannot control the tongues of gossips any more than you can control the wind." Charlotte pushed against his chest, creating space between them. "What of Beatrice? Have you considered how this would affect her? Or do your desires outweigh all other concerns?"

Edward's hands dropped to his sides, his anger deflating. "You think I haven't thought of these things? That I haven't lain awake nights wrestling with the implications?"

"Then you understand why this must end before it truly begins." Charlotte wrapped her arms around herself, as if seeking protection from her own feelings. "We cannot rewrite the rules of society, no matter how much we might wish to."

"Rules?" Edward laughed bitterly. "The same rules that trapped my sister in a loveless marriage? That force you to deny your heart for the sake of appearances?"

"At least my heart remains my own." Charlotte's words cut like steel. "Which is more than can be said for the women whose hearts you've collected and discarded."

Edward stepped closer again, his voice dropping to a dangerous whisper. "You know nothing of my heart, Charlotte. Nothing of the torment I've endured since your ingress. You claim to care for propriety, for reputation, yet you've ruined me more thoroughly than any scandal could."

"Then perhaps it's best we keep our distance," Charlotte replied, though her resolve wavered at his proximity. "Before we destroy everything—and everyone—we hold dear."

"And if I refuse to keep my distance?" Edward's hand rose to cup her cheek, his thumb brushing away a tear she hadn't realized had fallen. "If I choose to fight for what I want, consequences be damned?"

"Then you prove yourself exactly the man society believes you to be," Charlotte whispered, though she couldn't help leaning into his touch. "Selfish. Reckless. Uncaring of the damage you leave in your wake."

"No woman has ever refused me," Edward growled, stalking across the room like a caged tiger. "Not one."

"Then perhaps it's time someone did." Charlotte's voice quivered with barely controlled emotion. "We will not continue to lie together, Your Grace, nor will I become your mistress."

"Mistress?" Edward asked, genuine shock registering across his aristocratic features. His hands clenched at his sides as indignation coursed through him. "I have no desire to ask you to be that. The very thought offends me."

"What else could it be? Your reputation speaks for itself, Your Grace." Charlotte's voice held a bitter edge, though her heart thundered traitorously in her chest. The countless whispered tales of his conquests and dalliances echoed in her mind, each one a fresh wound to her already fragile hopes. "You can afford such cavalier attitudes, Your Grace. Your position protects you."

"While yours makes you a coward?"

"How dare you!" Charlotte's voice cracked with indignation. "You think it cowardly to protect my livelihood? My reputation? The peace of this household?"

"I think it cowardly to deny what's between us out of fear."

"And I think it selfish to pursue it out of desire."

"Selfish?" Edward laughed bitterly. "Yes, I suppose I am selfish. Selfish enough to want more than empty flirtations and meaningless conquests. Selfish enough to want you."

"You do not want me. You want what you cannot have."

"Do not presume to tell me what I want."

"Then do not presume to tell me what I should risk!"

"Risk?" His voice dropped dangerously low. "You speak of risk while standing there looking at me like that?"

"Like what?"

"Like you're fighting every instinct to step closer."

"Your arrogance knows no bounds."

"It isn't arrogance when it's truth. Your body betrays you, Charlotte. Your breathing quickens. Your cheeks flush. Your hands tremble."

"Stop it."

"Your lips part. Your pupils dilate. Every inch of you screams desire."

"I said stop!"

"Make me. Push me away. Tell me you feel nothing."

"You're impossible!"

"And you're intoxicating. Maddening. Unlike any woman I've ever known."

"Because I refuse you?"

"Because you challenge me. Match me. Drive me to distraction with a single glance."

"This is madness."

"Then let us be mad together."

"We can't."

"We can. We already have."

"That was a mistake."

"The only mistake is denying what we both know to be true."

"And what truth is that?"

"That I've never wanted anyone the way I want you."

"Want isn't enough."

"Then tell me what is!"

"Understanding. Respect. The wisdom to know that some lines should not be crossed."

"I respect you more than any woman I've ever known."

"Respect doesn't storm into a lady's chambers demanding satisfaction—"

The door burst open without warning. Lady Helena stood in the doorway, her face pale with shock and disappointment as she took in the scene before her—her brother looming over Charlotte, the governess pressed against the wall, both of them breathing heavily.

"Edward!" Helena's voice cracked like a whip. "What is the meaning of this?"

Edward stepped back as if burned, running a hand through his disheveled hair. "Helena, this isn't—"

"Isn't what?" Helena's eyes narrowed. "Isn't you taking advantage of my governess? Isn't you compromising her reputation and position in this household?"

"My lady," Charlotte pushed away from the wall, straightening her skirts with trembling hands. "Nothing improper has occurred between His Grace and myself."

"Do not insult my intelligence, Miss Larkspur." Helena's tone could have frozen flame. "I've seen the way you look at each other. The tension at dinner. And now I find my brother in your chambers after dark?"

"It was my fault entirely," Edward interjected. "Charlotte is blameless."

"Charlotte?" Helena's eyebrows rose at his familiar use of the governess's name. "So it's 'Charlotte' now, is it? How long has this been going on?"

"Nothing has been going on," Charlotte protested, her voice growing desperate. "Your Grace came here uninvited. I was just asking him to leave."

"That's not how it appeared from where I stand." Helena's gaze swept between them, hard as diamonds. "I heard raised voices. I saw his hands on you. Do not take me for a fool."

CHAPTER EIGHT
the dismissal

Rain lashed against the windows of Blackwood Estate, nature's fury matching the tumultuous emotions within. Lightning illuminated Lady Helena's private sitting room in brief, harsh flashes as she paced before the hearth, her fingers twisting together in distress.

"Mama, please!" Beatrice's voice cracked with desperation. She clung to her mother's skirts, tears streaming down her cherubic face. "Don't send Miss Charlotte away. She didn't do anything wrong!"

Helena's heart constricted at her daughter's plea. "My darling, sometimes adults must make difficult decisions to protect those we love." She stroked Beatrice's dark curls, though her own eyes glistened with unshed tears.

The door opened with quiet dignity, and Charlotte entered, her spine straight as steel despite the redness rimming her eyes. She wore her traveling cloak, a small valise clutched in her trembling hands.

"I've come to say goodbye, Miss Beatrice." Charlotte's voice remained steady, though emotion threatened to crack her composure.

Beatrice broke from her mother's embrace, flinging herself at Charlotte. "Please don't go! I'll be good, I promise!"

"You are already the most wonderful child." Charlotte knelt, gathering the sobbing girl close. "Never doubt that."

Charlotte's heart shattered anew with each sob that wracked Beatrice's small frame. Though her face remained composed, her soul cried out in anguish at the thought of leaving this precious child who had become so dear to her. The weight of Beatrice's arms around her neck felt like an anchor, threatening to break her resolve to depart with dignity.

"You must let go now, sweetling," Charlotte whispered, her voice thick with emotion as she disentangled herself from Beatrice's desperate embrace. Each step toward the door felt like walking through molasses, her legs leaden with grief.

In her chambers, Charlotte methodically packed her remaining belongings, her fingers trailing over the small tokens of her time at Blackwood Estate - a pressed flower Beatrice had given her, a ribbon from their first tea party together, a book of poetry she had often read in the gardens. Her mind wandered treacherously to the previous night's events, to Edward's fierce eyes blazing with anger and something darker, more dangerous. The memory of his cruel words still stung like fresh wounds.

"The Duke has already departed for London, miss," Martha, one of the housemaids, informed her as she helped carry Charlotte's trunk downstairs. "Left at first light, he did, before this dreadful weather set in."

Charlotte's breath caught in her throat. Of course he had fled - what else should she have expected from a man of his reputation? Still, the knowledge that he had not even deigned to face her after last night's confrontation twisted like a knife in her chest.

The rain drummed steadily against the cobblestones as footmen loaded her belongings into the waiting carriage. Charlotte pulled her cloak tighter, though the chill she felt came from within rather than without. As she settled into the worn leather seat, a flash of movement caught her eye.

There, pressed against the library window on the second floor, stood Beatrice. Her small hands splayed against the glass, tears streaming down her face as she waved frantically. Charlotte raised her own hand in response, her vision blurring as she struggled to memorize every detail of the child's beloved face.

The carriage lurched forward, and Charlotte pressed her fingertips to the cold window, watching as Beatrice's figure grew smaller and smaller. Her throat constricted with unshed tears as Blackwood Estate - the place that had briefly felt like home - began to disappear into the misty distance.

The steady rhythm of horses' hooves against wet earth matched the pounding of Charlotte's heart. Each beat seemed to whisper of what she was leaving behind: Beatrice's laughter echoing through the halls, the warmth of Lady Helena's initial kindness, and yes, even those stolen moments with Edward before everything had shattered like fine china dropped upon marble floors.

The rain streaked down the windows, distorting her view of the passing countryside. Charlotte found herself grateful for nature's veil, as if the weather itself sought to shield her from the full impact of her departure. Her fingers absently traced patterns in the condensation on the glass, much as she had done while teaching Beatrice her letters.

In her lap lay the letter of recommendation Lady Helena had pressed into her hands - proper, correct, and utterly devoid of warmth. The paper felt heavy with the weight of unspoken accusations and broken trust. Charlotte had not attempted to defend herself against Helena's assumptions. What could she say that would not sound like hollow protestations in the face of such damning circumstances?

The carriage rounded a bend in the road, and finally, finally, Charlotte allowed herself to weep. Silent tears rolled down her cheeks as she mourned not just the loss of her position, but the shattering of dreams she had barely allowed herself to acknowledge. Dreams of belonging, of family, of a love that might transcend the rigid boundaries of class and propriety.

EDWARD'S STALLION thundered through the gates of Blackwood Estate, hooves throwing mud in great arcs as he pulled the beast to an abrupt halt. His customary grace abandoned him as he practically fell from the saddle, tossing the reins to a startled stable boy.

"Your Grace!" The butler hurried forward, his usual composure slipping. "We did not expect—"

"What is it? What did you not expect?" Edward asked, removing his riding gloves. Sweat beaded at his temples, betraying the urgency of his arrival.

"It's Miss Larkspur," his butler said softly, knowing the chatter throughout the manor had spread like wildfire among the servants. The man's usual stoic demeanor wavered as he watched his master's face darken with concern, the riding gloves now crumpled in Edward's white-knuckled grip.

"What about her?" Edward's voice came out as a growl, his cravat askew and rain dripping from his coat. When the butler hesitated, Edward seized him by the shoulders. "What about Miss Larkspur?"

"My lord, Miss Larkspur departed not two hours past. Lady Helena—"

Edward didn't wait to hear more. He charged through the entrance hall, leaving muddy footprints across the marble floor. His heart pounded with a desperate rhythm that seemed to echo through his entire body. Helena had done it. His meddlesome, well-meaning sister had actually done it.

The parlor door burst open beneath his palm with such force it slammed against the wall. Helena sat primly in her favorite chair, her needlework spread across her lap as if this were any ordinary afternoon. She didn't even flinch at his dramatic entrance.

"How dare you?" The words tore from Edward's throat. "What right did you have to dismiss her?"

Helena set aside her embroidery with deliberate care. "I had every right, as the mother of an impressionable young girl and the sister of a man seemingly intent on destroying himself."

"Destroying myself?" Edward laughed, the sound harsh and bitter. "By what? Finding happiness with someone genuine for once in my life?"

"By pursuing a common governess and risking everything our family has built!" Helena's composure cracked slightly, her voice rising. "I heard you last night, Edward. The entire household heard you! What were you thinking, cornering her like that?"

Edward ran his fingers through his rain-dampened hair, his rage warring with shame at the memory of his behavior. "I was angry. I was... I wasn't thinking clearly."

"Precisely the problem." Helena stood, her eyes blazing with protective fury. "You never think clearly where lust is concerned. But I will not stand by and watch you throw away everything for a passing fancy."

"Helena—"

"The only way forward," Helena cut him off, "is for you to make a proper match. Miss Victoria Ashworth has shown considerable interest, and her family's connections would do much to stabilize our position in society."

Edward's laugh held no humor. "Miss Ashworth? That vapid, social-climbing—"

"That perfectly suitable young lady of our own class," Helena's voice cracked like a whip, "who could help restore your reputation and secure our family's future. Think of Beatrice, Edward. Think of her prospects if her uncle becomes known as the man who seduced her governess."

The words hit Edward like physical blows. He sank into a chair, the fight draining from him as quickly as it had come. "It was just once."

"One time too many," Helena's voice softened slightly. "But what other conclusion would society draw? What other conclusion could I draw, finding you alone with her, your voice raised in anger? There was ardor in your voice, Edward ... *passion*."

Edward closed his eyes, remembering Charlotte's face in that moment - hurt and dignity warring in her expression as she'd faced his tirade. Shame coursed through him anew.

"I know you mean well, Helena," he said at last, his voice rough. "But you don't understand what you've done."

"I understand perfectly." Helena moved to stand beside his chair, resting a gentle hand on his shoulder. "I understand that my brother, for all his faults, deserves a chance at real happiness. But it must be appropriate happiness, Edward. It must be with someone who can stand beside you as your equal in society's eyes."

Edward's heart constricted painfully in his chest. Every fiber of his being rebelled against the idea of pursuing Victoria Ashworth or any other society belle. Yet he could not deny the logic of Helena's words. The weight of his title, his responsibilities, his family's reputation - all of it pressed down upon him like a physical burden.

"Where did she go?" he asked quietly, already knowing Helena would not tell him.

"It's better you do not know." Helena squeezed his shoulder. "Better for both of you."

Edward stood abruptly, needing to move, to breathe, to escape the suffocating reality of his position. He strode to the window, watching the rain continue to fall. Somewhere out there, Charlotte was traveling away from him, probably believing the worst of him after last night. The thought was almost unbearable.

THE FOLLOWING AFTERNOON, Helena hosted a carefully orchestrated tea party in the front parlor. Victoria Ashworth sat in pride of place, her golden curls perfectly arranged, her rose-silk gown drawing admiring glances.

Edward slouched in his chair, radiating hostility. His teacup remained untouched as Victoria regaled the gathering with tales of her recent London season.

Edward studied Victoria Ashworth with the detached interest one might afford a particularly ornate piece of furniture. She possessed all the proper accouterments of a future duchess - golden hair arranged in fashionable curls, a complexion that spoke of careful attention to sun exposure, and clothing that whispered of wealth without shouting it. Even her laugh followed the prescribed social rhythm: gentle, musical, never too loud or too long.

"And then, Your Grace, Lady Winchester actually suggested we might arrange a musical evening." Victoria's voice floated across the space between them, practiced and precise. "I told her it would be delightful, though of course, one must be selective about the guest list."

Edward's fingers tightened around the delicate handle of his teacup. Everything about Miss Ashworth was correct, proper, and utterly suffocating. She knew exactly how to navigate the intricate maze of society, when to smile, when to demur, when to display just enough wit to be entertaining without threatening masculine sensibilities.

"Indeed," he managed, though his thoughts wandered to another woman who had never hesitated to challenge him, whose wit had cut through his pretenses like a freshly-honed blade.

Victoria preened under his apparent attention, misreading his distant expression for consideration. "I've always believed that music has such power to bring people together, don't you agree? Though some of the newer compositions are rather shocking in their passion."

The word 'passion' in Victoria's mouth sounded sterile, academic - nothing like the raw emotion that had thundered through his veins during that last confrontation with Charlotte. *Where was she now?* The question gnawed at him like a physical ache. Was she traveling through the rain-soaked countryside in some rattling coach? Had she found shelter at an inn, or perhaps reached whatever destination Helena had arranged?

"Your Grace?" Victoria's perfectly arranged features showed just the right amount of concern. "You seem rather distracted today."

Edward forced himself to focus on the woman before him. She was everything a duke's wife should be - well-connected, impeccably bred, thoroughly versed in the responsibilities that would come with the title of duchess. She would never cause a scandal, never challenge the established order, never make him question his own nature or actions.

"My apologies, Miss Ashworth. I find myself somewhat fatigued from recent business matters." The lie slipped easily from his lips, as smooth as the countless social pleasantries he'd mastered over the years.

"Oh, you must take care not to overtax yourself." Victoria's fan fluttered with practiced grace. "Perhaps a change of scene would be beneficial? The assembly rooms in Bath are particularly diverting this time of year."

The thought of enduring more structured social interactions made Edward's chest tighten. He imagined Charlotte's reaction to such a suggestion - the slight arch of her eyebrow, the barely concealed amusement in her eyes as she would have recognized his discomfort with such forced gaiety.

But Charlotte was gone, and here sat Miss Victoria Ashworth, the very model of what he should want. Their marriage would be a merger of titles and expectations, as smooth and emotionless as a business transaction. Their children would be raised with every advantage, their social position unassailable. It was the sensible choice, the right choice, the only choice if he wished to maintain his family's standing and secure Beatrice's future.

Yet his treacherous mind continued to conjure images of Charlotte - her face illuminated by candlelight as she read to Beatrice, her quiet dignity even in the face of his rage, the way her presence had somehow made Blackwood Estate feel more like a home than a showcase of wealth and privilege.

"Bath does have its charms," he replied mechanically, aware that too long a silence would be noted and commented upon.

Victoria's response about the relative merits of various social seasons washed over him like distant waves. Edward found himself tracking the movement of raindrops down the parlor windows, wondering if Charlotte was watching similar patterns elsewhere, perhaps thinking of him with disappointment or disdain. The uncertainty of her location and circumstances plagued him more than any business concern ever had.

"Don't you agree, Your Grace?" Victoria's musical laugh filled the room. "The theatre has become frightfully dull this year."

Edward's response was barely civil. "I wouldn't know, Miss Ashworth. I find artificial dramatics tedious."

Helena shot him a warning glance, while Victoria merely smiled, undeterred. "Perhaps you simply need the right companion to make such entertainment worthwhile."

In the corner, Beatrice sat listlessly, pushing her untouched cake around her plate. Her usual vibrant energy had dimmed to a shadow, her eyes constantly straying to the empty chair where Charlotte used to sit.

Victoria rose gracefully, moving to perch closer to Edward. "I've heard such fascinating things about your library, Your Grace. Might I trouble you for a tour?"

Edward's jaw clenched. "The library is not for public viewing."

"Surely you could make an exception?" Victoria's hand brushed his arm. "I'm particularly interested in your collection of Greek classics."

"The library is private." Edward stood abruptly, his chair scraping against the floor. "As are my thoughts on the matter."

Without another word, he strode from the room, leaving Victoria staring after him in shocked silence. The thunder of his footsteps echoed through the house, followed by the distant slam of a door that made the windows rattle in their frames.

CHAPTER NINE
revelations

A month of dreary days dragged by at Blackwood Estate, each sunrise bringing fresh attempts at diversion that proved increasingly hollow. Edward found himself trapped in an endless cycle of social obligations, hunt clubs, and tedious afternoons spent in Victoria Ashworth's company - all of which left him feeling more empty than the last.

The spring rains had finally ceased, leaving behind a landscape that should have felt renewed but instead seemed devoid of color. His proposal to Miss Ashworth had been perfunctory at best - a few practiced words delivered in her father's study with all the warmth of a business transaction. She had accepted, of course, with perfectly rehearsed joy that never reached her eyes.

Edward's thoughts drifted to their kiss from the previous evening. He had initiated it more out of curiosity than desire, wondering if any spark of passion might ignite between them. Victoria had remained still as marble beneath his touch, her lips cold and unyielding. Though she had made no move to stop him as his hands wandered, her mother's timely interruption had prevented matters from progressing further. In truth, he felt relieved at the intervention.

"What a farce this all is," he muttered, staring into his half-empty glass of brandy. The thought of bedding Victoria left him cold - she would likely lay there like a corpse, doing her duty with neither pleasure nor protest. An heir was all he needed from this union, nothing more. Yet the prospect filled him with a creeping dread that no amount of spirits could drown.

Through the window, he observed Helena in the garden with Beatrice and their new governess - a stern-faced woman who looked more suited to a prison than a schoolroom. His sister had declared herself satisfied with the arrangement, but Beatrice's usual vivacity had dimmed considerably. The child still asked for Miss Larkspur daily, her small face falling each time she was reminded that her beloved friend would not return.

"It's better this way," Edward told himself for the hundredth time, though the words rang hollow. Sending Charlotte away had been necessary - the scandal of their attraction would have ruined multiple lives. Yet her absence felt like a physical ache, a constant reminder of what he had lost. Or rather, what he had never truly possessed.

His fingers unconsciously traced the spot on his neck where Charlotte's breath had ghosted during their forbidden coition. The memory of her soft lips and passionate response haunted him still. Unlike Victoria's mechanical acceptance of his advances, Charlotte had met him with equal fervor, her body melting against his as though they were made to fit together.

Edward's grip tightened on his glass until his knuckles whitened. "Stop torturing yourself, you fool," he growled. There could be no future there - his duty to his title and family name demanded an appropriate match. Victoria

Ashworth, with her impeccable breeding and substantial dowry, was the logical choice. Love had nothing to do with it.

Still, in quiet moments like these, his mind inevitably wandered to Charlotte. *Where was she now? Did she think of him as often as he thought of her?* The urge to track her down, to see her face just once more, clawed at his chest with growing intensity. But he resisted, knowing that one glimpse would shatter his already fragile resolve.

Instead, he watched his sister and niece through the window, noting how Beatrice's shoulders slumped as the new governess barked out some instruction. Helena might claim satisfaction with the current state of affairs, but the price of propriety weighed heavily on them all. His hands were bound by duty and expectation, leaving him powerless to ease anyone's suffering - including his own.

The brandy burned his throat as he drained his glass, hoping to numb the persistent ache in his chest. Distance was the only solution, he reminded himself. In time, perhaps these feelings would fade. Charlotte would become nothing more than a bittersweet memory, and he would learn to be content with the life society demanded of him.

THE MORNING SUN cast long shadows across Edward's bedchamber as Cornwall, his trusted valet, helped him dress for the day. Edward stood before the mirror, lost in thought while Cornwall adjusted his cravat with practiced efficiency.

"Cornwall," Edward broke the companionable silence, his voice unusually hesitant. "Have you ever been in love?"

Cornwall's hands stilled on Edward's collar, surprise flickering across his weathered features. In ten years of service, the Duke had never inquired about his personal life.

"Yes, Your Grace. I have." Cornwall resumed his task, though his movements were more measured now.

Edward smirked, his azure eyes dancing with mischief as he studied his valet's reflection. "Your wife is lovely."

Cornwall smirked back, the weathered lines around his eyes crinkling with barely concealed amusement. "I did not say it was my wife, sir."

Edward's shoulders stiffened, and he met his servant's shocked gaze with one of his own. The playful atmosphere shifted into something more serious, more intimate. "Tell me."

"Sir?" Cornwall asked, his hands moving with practiced efficiency as he selected a pair of silver cufflinks from the ornate jewelry box. The morning light caught the polished metal, sending brief flashes across the bedchamber walls.

Edward met his valet's eyes in the mirror, his expression uncharacteristically vulnerable, almost boyish in its uncertainty. The usual mask of aristocratic indifference had slipped, revealing something raw beneath. "What is it like?"

Cornwall smoothed the fabric of Edward's jacket, considering his words carefully. "It's like discovering a part of yourself you never knew existed, Your Grace. Every moment feels more vivid, more alive. Even the simplest things—a shared glance across a room, the brush of hands—take on new meaning. But it's terrifying too, because suddenly your heart exists outside your own body, vulnerable to another's care."

Edward absorbed these words, his jaw tightening. "My duty does not involve love, Cornwall. The estate needs securing. The title needs an heir." He squared his shoulders. "I believe I must ask Miss Ashworth for her hand."

Cornwall paused in brushing invisible lint from Edward's sleeve. "Are you in love with Miss Ashworth, Your Grace?"

"No." The word fell between them, heavy with finality.

"Then might I suggest following your heart instead?"

Edward turned to face his valet directly. "Why would you suggest such a thing?"

A knowing look crossed Cornwall's face as he folded the discarded clothing. "Because, Your Grace, the housekeeper heard through whispers from the butler that they know where Miss Larkspur has gone."

Edward's breath caught, his carefully maintained composure cracking. His hands gripped the edge of the dressing table, knuckles white with tension as he processed this revelation.

Cornwall stood quietly, watching the war of emotions play across his master's features—hope warring with duty, desire with obligation. The morning light continued its slow crawl across the floor, marking the passage of time as Edward remained frozen in this moment of choice.

"Tell me," Edward commanded, his voice hoarse with barely contained emotion.

CORNWALL'S REVELATION left Edward pacing his chambers like a caged animal, his shoulders taut with nervous energy. She was sent to Bath - not three hours' journey from Blackwood Estate. The knowledge burned in his mind, an ember threatening to ignite into action.

"What good would it do?" he muttered, running agitated fingers through his dark hair. His reflection mocked him from the mirror - a man torn between desire and duty. Charlotte had maintained her silence since departing. No letters, no messages, not even a farewell note to Beatrice. Perhaps she had already moved forward, leaving behind their stolen moments as nothing more than a pleasant memory.

Yet the memory of her kiss haunted him still. His fingers absently traced his lips, remembering the softness of hers, the way she had melted against him in that darkened alcove. The ghost of her touch lingered on his skin, tormenting him with what could have been.

"Your Grace?" Cornwall's discrete cough interrupted his brooding. "Miss Ashworth has arrived. She awaits you in the morning room."

Edward's jaw clenched. Of course she had come - Victoria never missed an opportunity to stake her claim. With a resigned sigh, he straightened his cravat and descended to meet his intended.

Victoria stood by the window, a vision in pale blue silk that complemented her golden curls. She turned at his entrance, her practiced smile warming her features. "Edward, darling! I've had the most wonderful idea. There's to be a fair in Hyde Park tomorrow - all the ton will be there. We simply must attend."

Her enthusiasm grated against his melancholy mood. "I hardly think—"

"Oh, but we must!" Victoria glided closer, laying a delicate hand on his arm. "Everyone is so eager to see us together. Lady Winchester particularly mentioned how pleased she was about our engagement."

Edward fought the urge to shake off her touch. It felt wrong - too light, too calculated. Nothing like Charlotte's honest warmth. "I have business matters to attend to."

Victoria's lower lip protruded in a carefully crafted pout. "Surely those can wait? It would mean so much to me, Edward. I want everyone to see how happy we are."

Happy? The word tasted bitter in his mouth. But wasn't this exactly what he had chosen? A proper marriage, a suitable wife, all the trappings of his station? He had no right to complain about the very cage he had willingly entered.

"Perhaps..." Victoria's voice took on a thoughtful tone, "We could invite Lady Helena and dear Beatrice? It would be such a lovely family outing."

Edward's gaze snapped to her face, searching for signs of manipulation. But Victoria's expression remained earnest, if calculated. Including his sister and niece would certainly make the expedition more bearable. And Beatrice had been so withdrawn lately - perhaps an afternoon of entertainment would lift her spirits.

"Very well," he conceded, watching Victoria's face light up with triumph. "We shall all attend."

"Wonderful!" She clapped her hands together in delight. "I shall have my maid coordinate with Lady Helena about the arrangements. We'll make such a striking picture together, don't you think?"

Edward managed a noncommittal grunt, his thoughts already drifting back to Bath. To Charlotte. Would she be walking those elegant streets right now? Taking tea in the Pump Room? Reading to someone else's children with that gentle voice that had so captivated Beatrice?

"Edward?" Victoria's voice cut through his reverie. "Are you listening, darling?"

"Of course," he lied smoothly, though his heart remained leagues away. The fair would provide a welcome distraction, if nothing else. Perhaps amid the noise and spectacle, he could forget for a few hours that his soul yearned for a woman who was not, could never be, his bride.

CHAPTER TEN
a new role

Charlotte gazed out the window of Mrs. Stahlworth's elegant townhouse in Bath, watching raindrops trace lazy patterns down the glass. The autumn morning had dawned grey and dreary, but her employer's jovial nature brightened even the gloomiest of days.

"My dear, shall we venture to the Roman Baths today? I find myself in need of some ancient history to lift my spirits," Mrs. Stahlworth called from her favorite armchair, where she sat organizing her collection of theatre programs.

"Of course, though perhaps we ought to wait until the rain lessens." Charlotte turned from the window, grateful for the constant stream of diversions her new position provided. Mrs. Stahlworth's enthusiasm for life proved infectious, and Charlotte found herself swept along in the widow's pursuit of culture and entertainment.

"Nonsense! A little rain never hurt anyone. Besides, Ophelia is looking particularly forlorn today." Mrs. Stahlworth gestured to the potted fern she had named after Shakespeare's tragic heroine. "She could use the humidity."

Charlotte couldn't help but smile at her employer's whimsy. In the three months since she'd taken the position, she'd grown accustomed to Mrs. Stahlworth's habit of naming her plants after literary characters. The drawing room housed not only Ophelia but also Mercutio the peace lily and Portia the palm.

"Very well, I shall fetch our cloaks." Charlotte moved to the hallway, her steps lighter than they had been in weeks. The constant activity and Mrs. Stahlworth's warm companionship had begun to heal the raw edges of her heart.

As she reached for their outerwear, her fingers brushed against the soft fabric of her cloak, and unbidden, a memory surfaced - Edward's hands adjusting the hood around her face during their walk in the garden at Blackwood Estate. The phantom touch of his fingers against her chin made her breath catch.

She pushed the memory aside, focusing instead on the practical task of gathering their things. Yet as she helped Mrs. Stahlworth prepare for their outing, her mind wandered treacherously back to Edward. *Did he think of her?* Had he already moved forward with his duties, perhaps courting Miss Ashworth as society expected?

Charlotte pressed a hand to her temple, grateful that nature had followed its normal course after weeks of anxiety. The relief that flooded through her was profound - her reputation and livelihood remained intact. She could continue building her new life here in Bath without the specter of scandal haunting her steps.

"Are you quite well, my dear?" Mrs. Stahlworth peered at her with motherly concern as they made their way down the rain-slicked streets. "You look rather pale."

"Just a touch of feminine indisposition," Charlotte replied delicately. "Nothing to cause alarm."

Mrs. Stahlworth nodded knowingly. "Ah yes, I keep an excellent tea blend for such occasions. We shall have some when we return home."

Charlotte's shoulders relaxed, touched by the older woman's understanding. After the turmoil of recent months, she had found not just employment but genuine care in Mrs. Stahlworth's household. The weight that had pressed upon her chest since leaving Blackwood Estate lightened considerably.

She drew her cloak tighter against the autumn chill, remembering the sleepless nights spent praying her courses would arrive. The alternative would have meant absolute ruin - no respectable household would employ an unwed mother. All her years of building an impeccable reputation as a governess would have crumbled to dust.

"I'm thinking of hosting a small musical evening next week," Mrs. Stahlworth continued cheerfully. "Nothing grand - just a few friends to hear young Miss Palmer play the pianoforte. She's quite talented, though her mother insists on having her perform that dreadful Hungarian march at every gathering."

Charlotte smiled, grateful for the distraction. "Perhaps we could suggest something by Mozart instead? His sonatas are always well received."

As they approached the entrance to the Roman Baths, Charlotte's thoughts drifted again to Edward. The passion they had shared in that darkened alcove seemed like a dream now - beautiful but dangerous. Thank heaven she had escaped before their indiscretion could bear more permanent consequences.

She straightened her spine, reminding herself that she had made the right choice in leaving. A governess could not afford to indulge in romantic fantasies about her employer's brother, no matter how compelling he might be. She had her reputation to protect, her future to secure.

Mrs. Stahlworth continued chattering about her planned soirée as they descended the steps into the ancient baths. The steam rising from the water created an otherworldly atmosphere, and Charlotte breathed deeply of the mineral-scented air. Here in this timeless place, her own troubles seemed to diminish.

"Now then," Mrs. Stahlworth said, settling onto a bench overlooking the main pool, "shall we discuss what's truly troubling you? I may be advanced in years, my dear, but I recognize heartache when I see it."

Charlotte's carefully maintained composure wavered. "I... I would rather not speak of it."

"Sometimes silence merely gives our fears more power." Mrs. Stahlworth patted the space beside her. "Come, sit with me awhile."

Tears pricked at Charlotte's eyes as she sank onto the bench. The relief of the morning had unleashed emotions she had kept tightly controlled for weeks. Her voice trembled as she spoke, "I have been such a fool."

"Love rarely makes wise men or women of any of us," Mrs. Stahlworth replied gently. "But foolishness passes, my dear. The heart heals, and we grow stronger for having dared to feel deeply."

The kindness in the older woman's voice nearly undid Charlotte's composure entirely. She pulled her handkerchief from her sleeve, dabbing at her eyes. "I cannot afford such luxury of feeling. My position - my very livelihood - depends upon maintaining proper boundaries."

THE DAYS WERE EASIER NOW, filled with Mrs. Stahlworth's endless pursuits of knowledge and culture. They visited museums, attended lectures, and explored the city's architectural wonders. Charlotte found herself genuinely engaged in their adventures, her natural curiosity awakening under Mrs. Stahlworth's enthusiastic guidance.

But the nights - *oh*, the nights were another matter entirely. In the quiet darkness of her chamber, Charlotte could not escape the memories of Edward's touch, the intensity of his gaze, the way his presence had filled every room he entered. She would lie awake, remembering the stolen moment in the alcove, the press of his lips against hers, the overwhelming sense of rightness she'd felt in his arms.

"Charlotte?" Mrs. Stahlworth's voice once again pulled her from her thoughts. "The carriage is ready."

Charlotte nodded, gathering her composure. She helped Mrs. Stahlworth down the front steps, holding an umbrella over them both as they made their way to the waiting carriage. The older woman's cherry-red cloak brightened the grey morning, much like her personality brightened Charlotte's days.

As they settled into the carriage, Mrs. Stahlworth produced a book of Roman history from her reticule. "Perhaps you could read to me on the journey? My eyes aren't what they used to be in this light."

Charlotte accepted the volume gratefully, knowing the activity would keep her mind occupied. She began to read aloud, her voice steady despite the tumult in her heart. The words flowed easily, filling the carriage with tales of ancient civilizations and long-lost empires.

Yet even as she read, a part of her mind wandered to Blackwood Estate, to Beatrice's sweet face and Edward's compelling presence. The ache in her chest had become a familiar companion, as constant as her breath, as steady as her heartbeat. During the day, she could almost convince herself she was healing, moving forward, finding purpose in her new life. But her heart knew better - it remembered everything, every glance, every word, every touch.

A WEEK LATER, the autumn sun cast long shadows across the cobblestones as Mrs. Stahlworth bustled into the morning room, her face alight with excitement. Charlotte looked up from her needlework, recognizing the telltale signs of another adventure brewing in her employer's mind.

"My dear, have you heard? There's to be a magnificent fair in Hyde Park. All of Bath is absolutely abuzz with talk of it." Mrs. Stahlworth adjusted her lorgnette, though she forgot to actually peer through it. "We simply must attend."

Charlotte's fingers stilled on her embroidery. The thought of such a public gathering made her stomach clench. *What if he were there?* The possibility, however remote, sent her heart racing. "Perhaps we might find a quieter pursuit for the afternoon?"

"Nonsense! Romeo is positively wilting from lack of entertainment." Mrs. Stahlworth gestured to the rather healthy-looking rose bush in the corner. "Besides, I hear they've brought performers from the Continent. Imagine - real French acrobats!"

Charlotte set aside her needlework, smoothing her skirts as she considered how to decline gracefully. Yet one look at Mrs. Stahlworth's eager expression made her resolve waver. The older woman had shown her such kindness, offering not just employment but genuine friendship when she needed it most.

"I suppose a brief visit couldn't hurt," Charlotte conceded, though her mind whirled with possibilities. *Would news of her presence at the fair reach London? Would it matter if it did?*

"Splendid! I shall have Thompson prepare the carriage." Mrs. Stahlworth clapped her hands in delight. "Do wear that lovely blue muslin of yours. It brings out the warmth in your eyes."

As her employer swept from the room, Charlotte pressed her hands to her cheeks, feeling the heat beneath her palms. The prospect of attending such a public event sent anxiety coursing through her veins. Since arriving in Bath, she'd carefully avoided large gatherings, preferring the quiet companionship of Mrs. Stahlworth and their small circle of acquaintances.

You're being ridiculous, she chided herself. *He won't be there. He's likely in London, fulfilling his duties, courting some suitable lady of the ton.* The thought brought both relief and a sharp stab of pain.

An hour later, Charlotte found herself seated beside Mrs. Stahlworth in the carriage, wearing the blue muslin as requested. The older woman chattered happily about the fair's attractions, while Charlotte's mind wandered treacherously to the last fair she'd attended - at Blackwood Estate, where Edward had won a ribbon for his horsemanship.

"You're miles away, my dear," Mrs. Stahlworth observed, patting Charlotte's hand. "Is something troubling you?"

"Not at all," Charlotte replied, forcing a smile. "I was merely thinking about the weather. It's quite perfect for an outing."

Mrs. Stahlworth's knowing look suggested she wasn't fooled, but she kindly redirected the conversation to the latest scandal involving the local assembly rooms' master of ceremonies and a missing wig.

As their carriage joined the steady stream of vehicles heading toward Hyde Park, Charlotte's apprehension grew. The fair would undoubtedly draw society from all corners of Bath and perhaps beyond. *What if someone recognized her? What if word got back to Lady Helena?*

"Oh, look at the crowds!" Mrs. Stahlworth exclaimed as they approached. "Isn't it wonderful to see so many people enjoying themselves?"

Charlotte nodded mutely, her throat tight with anxiety. The fairground sprawled before them, a riot of color and sound. Vendors called their wares, children darted between stalls, and ladies in their finest promenaded along the paths, parasols twirling above their heads.

As Thompson helped them descend from the carriage, Charlotte took a deep breath, steadying herself. *You're being silly,* she told herself firmly. *This is Bath, not London. You're here to ensure Mrs. Stahlworth's enjoyment, nothing more.*

Yet as they made their way into the crowd, Charlotte couldn't help but scan the faces around her, her heart jumping at every tall, dark-haired gentleman who passed. Each false recognition left her both relieved and strangely disappointed, a contradiction that only served to frustrate her further.

Mrs. Stahlworth's enthusiasm, however, proved impossible to resist. The older woman's delight in every sight and sound gradually drew Charlotte out of her shell. They sampled candied almonds, applauded the French acrobats, and admired the displays of local craftsmanship.

"Shall we visit the fortune teller?" Mrs. Stahlworth suggested, pointing to a brightly colored tent. "Juliet would never forgive me if we didn't seek a glimpse of the future." She nodded toward the potted geranium waiting at home.

Charlotte hesitated. The thought of having her fortune told, of possibly hearing predictions about love and marriage, made her pulse quicken uncomfortably. *What if the fortune teller saw the truth in her heart? What if she spoke of a dark-haired duke and impossible dreams?*

Charlotte sat beside Mrs. Stahlworth on a shaded bench, grateful for the gentle rustling of leaves that offered respite from the afternoon sun.

"My dear, would you read the next passage? The one about the knight's quest?" Mrs. Stahlworth adjusted her lorgnette, squinting at the pages of their shared novel.

Charlotte's voice faltered mid-sentence as her gaze caught on a familiar figure in the distance.

It was *him*.

The Duke of Blackwood stood tall and commanding, his presence drawing attention even amid the bustling crowd. On his arm, Miss Victoria Ashworth sparkled like a jewel, her golden hair catching the sunlight as she laughed at something he had said.

"Charlotte?" Mrs. Stahlworth followed her companion's line of sight. "Ah, what a lovely pair they make."

Charlotte nodded her head as Mrs. Stahlworth continued.

"The Duke of Blackwood and his betrothed. Have you seen the announcement in the papers? Quite the match, they say. Though between us, I find Miss Ashworth rather too pleased with herself."

The words struck Charlotte like physical blows, each one landing precisely where her heart had already cracked. She forced her features into a mask of polite interest, though her fingers trembled as she closed the book in her lap.

"Lovely, indeed," Charlotte managed, her voice steady despite the hollow ache in her chest.

Mrs. Stahlworth shifted on the bench, her eyes bright with interest. "Oh, those candied nuts smell divine. Would you be a dear and fetch some for me? My old bones protest at too much walking today."

Charlotte welcomed the escape, rising perhaps too quickly from the bench. She moved through the crowd, each step carrying her further from the sight of Edward - the Duke, she corrected herself firmly - and his future duchess.

"Miss Charlotte! Miss Charlotte!"

The high-pitched cry of delight preceded the small figure that barreled into her skirts. Beatrice's face beamed up at her, joy radiating from every feature.

"My darling girl," Charlotte whispered, gathering the child close. The familiar weight of Beatrice in her arms brought tears to her eyes. "I've missed you so very much."

"Miss Larkspur." Lady Helena's voice cut through the moment like a knife. Behind her stood a tall, severe-looking woman Charlotte assumed was Beatrice's new governess. "What an unexpected pleasure."

Charlotte curtsied gracefully, her movements practiced and precise from years of propriety. She ran her delicate hand through Beatrice's silken hair, smoothing the dark strands that had escaped during the child's enthusiastic greeting. With tender care, she adjusted the pale pink bow that had come loose in their embrace, her fingers deftly retying the satin ribbon until it sat perfectly against the little girl's head once more.

She gave the new governess a stern look.

Helena's eyes darted anxiously over Charlotte's shoulder, and her next words tumbled out in a rush. "We really must be going. Come along, Beatrice."

"But Mama—"

"Now, Beatrice."

Charlotte watched her former employer, the new governess and Beatrice walking away. Her heart continued to ache.

Charlotte turned toward the candied nut vendor, her movements mechanical as she purchased Mrs. Stahlworth's treats. The paper cone felt rough against her fingertips as she made her way back through the crowd.

Time seemed to slow as she approached the path that would lead her back to Mrs. Stahlworth's bench. And there he stood, just a few feet away. The Duke of Blackwood stood regal with Miss Ashworth's hand possessively curved around his arm.

His eyes met Charlotte's, and for a breath, the sounds of the fair faded away.

The Duke inclined his head slightly - a gesture appropriate between slight acquaintances, nothing more. Charlotte returned the courtesy with a shallow curtsy, her gaze sliding past him as though he were indeed a stranger.

CHAPTER ELEVEN
the fair at hyde park

Charlotte's steps carried her swiftly through the crowd, each footfall a desperate attempt to escape the image now seared into her mind. Three months of careful distance, of building walls around her heart brick by painful brick, and one glimpse of Edward had sent them crumbling like sand.

She'd grown accustomed to his absence in her daily life. The mornings no longer held that sharp sting of knowing she wouldn't see him in the breakfast room, wouldn't catch his eye across the table as Beatrice regaled them with her dreams. The evenings had lost that hollow ache of missing his presence in the library, where they'd once shared quiet moments discussing literature and life.

But seeing him now, so close she could have reached out and touched the fabric of his perfectly tailored coat, awakened every dormant feeling she'd tried to bury. The way his eyes still held that intensity, the slight quirk of his mouth as he listened to Miss Ashworth's animated chatter - these details hit Charlotte with the force of a physical blow.

Stop this foolishness, she chided herself, weaving between groups of fairgoers with barely a murmured apology. *You knew this would happen. You knew he would marry someone of his own class.*

Miss Ashworth did look radiantly happy, her golden curls bouncing with each delighted laugh, her gloved hand placed just so on Edward's arm. Of course she was happy - she'd won the greatest prize of the Season. The notorious Duke of Blackwood, finally caught and tamed. What debutante wouldn't be thrilled with such a victory?

Good for her, Charlotte thought, the words tasting bitter even in her mind. *She'll make him a proper duchess. She knows all the right people, all the correct ways to behave. She'll never embarrass him at ton gatherings or make him question his place in society.*

The candied nuts Mrs. Stahlworth had requested lay forgotten in Charlotte's hand as she pushed through the crowd, no destination in mind except *away*. She couldn't bear another moment of watching Edward and his intended, couldn't stomach the sight of Miss Ashworth's proprietary smile or the way Edward bent his head to catch her words.

The sounds of the fair grew distant as Charlotte found herself in a quieter corner of the grounds. Her chest heaved with barely contained emotion, and she pressed a hand against her stays, willing her heart to slow its frantic beating.

You knew this day would come, she reminded herself. *You've had months to prepare.*

But no amount of preparation could have steeled her against the reality of seeing the Duke of Blackwood with his future bride. The pain felt fresh and raw, as if she were leaving Blackwood Estate all over again.

. . .

BACK AT THEIR BENCH, Mrs. Stahlworth watched Charlotte's retreat with growing concern. Her companion's face had gone white as chalk, her usual grace replaced by barely contained desperation as she fled the scene. In that moment, Mrs. Stahlworth understood with perfect clarity why Charlotte had been so reluctant to attend the fair.

The older woman's sharp eyes hadn't missed the exchange between Charlotte and the Duke, brief though it was. Nor had she missed the way the Duke's shoulders had tensed at the sight of her companion, or how his carefully composed expression had flickered for just a moment.

So that's the way of it, Mrs. Stahlworth thought, her heart aching for the young woman who had brought such joy to her household. She'd suspected there was more to Charlotte's story than a simple change of employment, but the depth of pain she'd glimpsed in those few seconds told a far more complex tale.

Mrs. Stahlworth gripped her lorgnette tightly, torn between following Charlotte immediately and giving her a moment to compose herself. She watched as the Duke of Blackwood's betrothed tugged him toward a display of imported silks, her tinkling laugh carrying across the fairground. The Duke moved as if pulled by strings, his attention clearly elsewhere despite Miss Ashworth's animated chatter.

CHARLOTTE'S PAIN radiated from her in waves as she pressed her back against a tree trunk, hidden from the main thoroughfare. The rough bark caught at the delicate fabric of her blue muslin, but she barely noticed. Her mind whirled with memories she'd tried so hard to suppress - Edward's smile when she challenged his opinions, the warmth in his eyes when he watched her with Beatrice, the way his hand had trembled slightly when he'd touched her face in the alcove.

The weight of the day's revelations pressed against Charlotte's chest like a physical force as she stood motionless behind the tree. Her fingers curled into the rough bark, seeking an anchor against the tide of emotions threatening to sweep her away.

Engaged. The word echoed through her mind with the finality of a death knell. She had known, of course, that Edward would marry eventually. It was his duty as the Duke of Blackwood to secure an heir, to maintain the family line. But knowing something would happen and witnessing it firsthand were entirely different matters.

Charlotte closed her eyes, but the image of Edward and Miss Ashworth remained, branded into her consciousness. They had looked... proper together. A duke and his future duchess, both born and bred to their positions in society. Miss Ashworth's golden curls and fashionable gown spoke of wealth and breeding, everything Charlotte could never offer.

"Charlotte?" Mrs. Stahlworth's concerned voice carried across the grass. "My dear, where have you gone?"

Charlotte straightened, hastily brushing at her skirts. "Here, Mrs. Stahlworth. I apologize for my lengthy absence." Her voice sounded strange to her own ears, as if it belonged to someone else entirely.

The older woman's shrewd eyes took in Charlotte's pale face and trembling hands. "I believe we've had quite enough fresh air for one day. Shall we return home?"

Home. The word struck Charlotte with unexpected force. Once, *home* had meant Blackwood Estate, with its sprawling gardens and library filled with first editions. *Home* had meant Beatrice's laughter echoing through the halls and stolen glances across dinner tables. Now, *home* was Mrs. Stahlworth's modest townhouse, comfortable but lacking the warmth of memory.

Their carriage ride passed in silence, Mrs. Stahlworth mercifully refraining from comment as Charlotte stared unseeing at the London streets sliding past. The announcement must have appeared in the papers - how had she missed it? Had she been so determined to avoid any news of Edward that she'd blinded herself to reality?

Upon reaching the townhouse, Charlotte excused herself immediately. "I find I have a headache coming on," she murmured, not meeting Mrs. Stahlworth's knowing gaze. "If you'll permit me to retire early..."

"Of course, my dear. Rest well."

The stairs to her chamber had never seemed so long. Each step required monumental effort, as if her shoes were filled with lead. When she finally reached her room, Charlotte closed the door with exquisite care before allowing her composure to crack.

The tears came silently at first, then in great, heaving sobs that shook her entire frame. She pressed her face into her pillow, muffling the sound of her grief. All the emotions she'd suppressed over the past months poured out of her: longing, regret, anger at herself for caring so deeply about a man who could never be hers.

You fool, she berated herself. *You utter, complete fool. Did you think he would pine for you forever? Did you imagine he would throw away his duties, his position, his entire world for a governess?*

But oh, how it hurt to see him again. To witness the easy way Miss Ashworth touched his arm, claimed his attention. Had he looked at the golden-haired beauty the way he'd once looked at

Charlotte? Did his breath catch when their eyes met across crowded rooms?

Charlotte rolled onto her back, staring at the darkening ceiling as tears tracked silently down her temples. Tomorrow, she would compose herself. Tomorrow, she would smile and read to Mrs. Stahlworth and pretend her heart hadn't been shattered all over again. But tonight... tonight she would allow herself this weakness, this indulgence in grief for all that might have been.

The moon rose slowly outside her window, casting silver shadows across her bed. Her pillow grew damp with tears as memories assaulted her: Edward's laugh during their walks in the garden, the warmth of his hand when he'd helped her from carriages, the intensity in his eyes during their last encounter in the alcove. Each recollection was a fresh wound, adding to the ache in her chest until breathing itself became an act of courage.

I must forget him, she thought fiercely, even as fresh tears spilled from her eyes. *I must lock away these feelings and move forward. I must.*

But in the sanctuary of her darkened chamber, with only the moon as witness, Charlotte knew the truth: she would never forget Edward Ashcombe, Duke of Blackwood. He had marked her heart as surely as if he'd branded it, and no amount of time or distance would erase that mark.

CHAPTER TWELVE
spoiled no more

The autumn wind rattled against the library windows of Blackwood Estate as Edward stood motionless, staring out at the grounds below. His fingers traced absent patterns on the glass, much like his thoughts traced back to that day in Hyde Park. Charlotte's face, her gentle eyes meeting his across the crowd, haunted him still.

"Damn it all," he muttered, turning to pour himself another glass of brandy. The liquid burned his throat, but failed to scorch away the memory of her.

The grand house felt more like a prison now, its elegant corridors echoing with Victoria's persistent attempts to gain his attention. His new wife - the thought made him grimace.

Edward paced the length of his private chambers, the memories of his wedding night with Victoria plaguing his thoughts like a persistent shadow. The brandy glass dangled precariously from his fingers as he recalled the awkward fumbling in the darkness, her nervous questions breaking every moment of potential passion.

"Edward?" she had whispered, her voice trembling. "Should I—is this—?" The constant stream of uncertainties had grated on his nerves, each question driving another nail into the coffin of desire.

He drained his glass, hoping the burn of alcohol might chase away the recollection of her rigid form beneath him, as unyielding as a marble statue. Victoria had laid there, eyes wide with trepidation, her responses mechanical and reserved. Nothing like the passion he had imagined with—

No. He would not allow his mind to venture down that path.

The bed sheets had rustled with uncomfortable tension as Victoria attempted to position herself according to what she'd been told by her mother. The sound had reminded Edward of dead leaves skittering across stone. When he'd tried to kiss her neck, she'd giggled nervously, destroying any semblance of ardor he'd managed to build.

"Is this proper?" she'd asked, breaking his concentration yet again. "Mother said—"

Edward's fingers tightened around the empty glass. He'd wanted to snap that her mother had no place in their bedchamber, but he'd held his tongue. Instead, he'd forced himself to be gentle, to be patient, to fulfill his ducal duty with as much consideration as he could muster.

The entire affair had been clinical, devoid of the fire he craved. Victoria's tentative touches had felt like butterfly wings against his skin – too light, too hesitant, too innocent. He'd found himself gritting his teeth through the entire ordeal, thinking only of securing his lineage rather than finding any pleasure in the act.

Afterward, when Victoria had reached for him with questioning fingers and whispered, "Might we... again?" he'd already been halfway out of bed. The thought of enduring another round of her anxious inquiries and rigid responses had been more than he could bear.

"Rest," he'd commanded, perhaps more harshly than necessary, pulling on his robe. "You'll need your strength for tomorrow."

Now, standing in the shadows of his chamber, Edward felt the weight of his choices pressing down upon him. The marriage bed, which should have been a sanctuary of passion and connection, had become yet another obligation to endure. Victoria's naive attempts at seduction in the days since had only served to drive him further into isolation.

He'd caught her studying a book of poetry yesterday, no doubt hoping to glean some insight into romance. The sight had twisted something inside him – not because of her efforts, but because he remembered another woman who had quoted Shakespeare with natural grace, who had understood the power of words without having to study them.

A knock at his door interrupted his brooding. "Your Grace?" Victoria's muffled voice carried through the wood. "Might I join you this evening?"

Edward's jaw clenched. The thought of another night of her hesitant touches and endless questions made him reach for the brandy decanter once more. "I have correspondence to attend to," he called back, the lie tasting bitter on his tongue. "Perhaps another time."

He heard her soft sigh, followed by the whisper of her slippers on the carpet as she retreated. The sound of her departure brought equal measures of relief and self-loathing. What kind of man avoided his own wife's bed? But the thought of facing another night like their wedding night, with its awkward silences and mechanical movements, made his skin crawl.

The brandy sloshed in his glass as he resumed his pacing. Victoria tried – he couldn't fault her for that. She followed every rule of propriety, every guideline her mother had undoubtedly drilled into her head about being a proper wife. But therein lay the problem. She was trying to be what she thought he wanted, rather than simply being.

She had given him what he needed: legitimacy, respectability, and now an heir growing in her womb. Yet each night when she reached for him, her touch felt like ice against his skin.

In his darkest moments, alone in his study, Edward tortured himself with thoughts of what might have been. He should have claimed Charlotte that night in her room—consequences be damned. The scandal would have forced their marriage, and at least then he would have known the warmth of true passion. But the thought of Helena's disappointment, of little Beatrice facing society's cruel whispers, had stayed his hand.

"Your Grace?" A servant's voice interrupted his brooding. "Lady Helena asks if you'll join the family for dinner this evening."

Edward waved his hand dismissively. "Send my regrets. I have business to attend to."

The lie came easily now, as did avoiding his sister's concerned glances and attempts at conversation. Helena tried, god knows she tried, to draw him out of his self-imposed isolation. Her gentle inquiries about his welfare, her careful suggestions that perhaps he might try to find happiness with Victoria - all met with stony silence or curt dismissals.

Even Beatrice, sweet Beatrice who once brought such joy to his days, could not penetrate the walls he'd built around himself. Just yesterday, she had burst into his study, eager to show him a new drawing. He'd barely glanced at it before making some excuse about important correspondence.

The hurt in her eyes had been unbearable, but still preferable to the memories her presence stirred - memories of Charlotte teaching Beatrice in the garden, their shared laughter carried on the summer breeze.

Victoria's pregnancy progressed, and with it, Edward's relief grew. Soon she would give him an heir, fulfilling her duty as he had fulfilled his. He had withdrawn from her bed completely, ignoring her tears and pleas. He knew it was cruel, but the thought of touching her, of pretending she was the woman he truly wanted, had become unbearable.

Each night as he lay alone in his chambers, Edward would close his eyes and see Charlotte's face. He imagined her soft skin beneath his fingers, her sweet voice whispering his name. The fantasy sustained and tormented him in equal measure.

"Just a few more months," he murmured to himself, watching as the autumn leaves swirled past his window. A few more months until the birth of his son—for it must be a son—and then his duty would be complete. He could retreat further into himself, let the world believe him to be merely an eccentric nobleman more interested in his business affairs than his young wife.

But oh, how his heart ached for Charlotte. The memory of her in Hyde Park, their eyes meeting across the crowd, haunted his dreams. She had looked beautiful, composed, everything he remembered and more. And he had been forced to walk past her with Victoria on his arm, playing the part of the devoted husband-to-be.

The brandy glass in his hand shattered, and Edward looked down in surprise at his bloodied fingers. He hadn't realized he'd been gripping it so tightly. As he watched the blood drip onto his pristine cravat, he thought it rather fitting—a physical manifestation of his internal wounds.

Helena's soft footfalls went unnoticed as she entered the library, but the sharp intake of her breath cut through the heavy silence when she spotted the blood dripping from Edward's hand. Without hesitation, she rushed to the corner cabinet where their father had always kept medical supplies, her skirts rustling as she moved with practiced efficiency.

"Edward, what have you done?" She pulled out clean linen and a small bottle of spirits, hurrying back to her brother's side. The shattered remnants of his brandy glass littered the floor around his feet, catching the dying light like fallen stars.

Before she could begin tending to his wound, Edward's bloodied hand shot out, grasping her wrist. His eyes, usually so guarded, now brimmed with unshed tears as they met hers. The raw anguish she saw there made her heart clench.

"Why must each day be filled with torment?" His voice cracked on the last word, and Helena felt her own eyes growing damp in response.

"Come," she said softly, guiding him away from the broken glass toward the plush leather sofa. They sank down together, and Helena noticed how her brother's normally perfect posture had crumpled, as if the weight of his pain was physically pressing him down.

Edward's shoulders began to shake, and Helena wrapped her arms around him as she had done when they were children and he'd fallen from his pony. But this was no simple tumble that could be soothed with sweet treats and kind words. This was a man's heart *breaking*.

"I still love her, Helena," he confessed, his words muffled against her shoulder. "God help me, I love Charlotte with every breath I take. Victoria…" He pulled back, wiping roughly at his eyes with his uninjured hand. "I do not love her. I will *never* love her. Each time she reaches for me, I feel as though I'm betraying the only woman who has ever truly touched my heart."

Helena's hand moved in gentle circles on his back as she listened. Her own heart ached for her brother's pain, for the impossible situation they had all found themselves in. She thought of Charlotte's quiet dignity, of Victoria's growing belly, of the twisted path that had led them here.

"Losing love," Helena said carefully, drawing from her own well of grief, "is like death, Edward. The pain…" She paused, gathering her thoughts. "The pain never truly leaves us. But we learn to carry it differently. You can still love Charlotte without being with her physically. Keep your memories of her cherished, hidden in your heart where they cannot hurt anyone else."

Edward cleared his throat roughly, swiping at his tears with his uninjured hand. His voice emerged hoarse, barely above a whisper. "Do you truly believe what you say, Helena? That this pain will become… manageable?"

Helena's heart ached as she watched her normally composed brother struggle for control. The flickering firelight cast shadows across his face, highlighting the dark circles beneath his eyes and the new lines etched around his mouth. She reached for his injured hand, beginning to clean and wrap it with gentle movements.

"I believe," she said carefully, "that time gives us perspective. When George died, I thought the weight of my grief would crush me. But look at me now—I can speak of him without falling apart. I still love him, still miss him, but I've learned to carry that love differently."

Edward's bitter laugh cut through the air. "Perhaps this is my comeuppance. How many hearts have I carelessly broken over the years? How many women have I left behind without a second thought?" He pulled his bandaged hand away from Helena's grasp, flexing his fingers. "The great Duke of Blackwood, finally brought low by love."

"Edward—" Helena began, but he cut her off.

"No, sister, let me speak. All my life, I've been granted every wish, every whim. If I desired something, it was mine for the taking." He stood abruptly, pacing before the fire. "But the one thing—the one person I truly want, I cannot have. The cruelty of it..." His voice cracked. "The absolute cruelty of it is that I finally understand what love truly means, and I'm bound to another."

Helena watched him move, her own thoughts turning inward. *Oh, Charlotte,* she mused silently, *I sent you away thinking to protect my family's reputation, to shield Beatrice from scandal. But at what cost?* She remembered her daughter's tearful pleas to keep her beloved governess, the way Beatrice still asked for Charlotte during bedtime stories.

Perhaps, Helena thought, *I should write to some of my connections. Discreetly inquire after Charlotte's situation. Surely there must be some way to ease this pain for all of us.* Her fingers itched to pick up a quill, to begin reaching out to her vast network of society acquaintances. She had always prided herself on maintaining correspondence with the right people—now those connections might prove useful in an unexpected way.

"You're thinking rather loudly, sister," Edward observed, pausing in his pacing to study her face. "I recognize that look. You're plotting something."

Helena smoothed her skirts, choosing her words carefully. "I was merely thinking that perhaps some correspondence is in order. Not to change anything, mind you, but to... ease certain burdens."

Edward's eyes narrowed. "Helena—"

"I won't meddle," she assured him quickly. "But surely knowing that Charlotte is well, that she is safe and comfortable... wouldn't that bring you some peace?"

He sank back onto the sofa beside her, running his good hand through his already disheveled hair. "I'm not certain anything can bring me peace now. Not with Victoria..." He trailed off, unable to speak of his wife's condition.

Helena reached for his hand again, squeezing it gently. "You're not being punished, Edward. Life simply... life simply is what it is sometimes. We make choices, and we must live with them. But that doesn't mean we can't find ways to make the burden lighter."

Edward's shoulders slumped, and when he spoke, his voice carried all the weariness of his soul. "And what of my child? What kind of father can I be when I feel nothing but resentment toward its mother? When each time I look at Victoria, I see only what I've lost?"

Helena held her brother for a long moment, feeling the tension in his shoulders, the way his breathing hitched with barely suppressed emotion. How different he was now from the carefree rake who had scandalized London society with his exploits. Love had transformed him, but at what cost?

She remembered him as a boy, always getting his way—their parents indulging his every whim while she watched from the sidelines. Even then, she had enabled him, covering for his misdeeds, making excuses for his behavior. Perhaps if she had been stricter, had forced him to face consequences earlier...

But no. Such thoughts served no purpose now.

"Rest, Edward," she murmured, pulling back to study his face. The shadows beneath his eyes spoke of sleepless nights, and his usual immaculate appearance had grown careless. Her heart ached to see him so diminished.

He managed a weak smile, though it didn't reach his eyes. "You needn't worry about me, Helena."

"I am your sister. Worrying about you is my prerogative." She smoothed his cravat, a habitual gesture from their childhood. "Try to get some sleep tonight. Brandy helps."

His only response was a noncommittal grunt as he turned back to the window, dismissing her presence. Helena sighed inwardly. How many times had she witnessed this pattern? His retreat into himself, the walls he built to keep others from seeing his pain. She had allowed it before, thinking it better to let him work through his moods alone.

But this was different. This wasn't some passing fancy or thwarted desire. This was love—true, deep, transformative love—and it had changed her brother in ways she was only beginning to understand.

As she made her way to her private sitting room, Helena's mind raced with possibilities. Her correspondence desk stood ready, paper and ink waiting. She had connections throughout London society, discrete friends who might be persuaded to make subtle inquiries about Charlotte's whereabouts and situation.

Settling into her chair, Helena pulled out her finest stationery. The scratch of her quill against paper filled the quiet room as she composed her first letter to Lady Worthington, a dowager known for her extensive network of social connections. Another would go to Mrs. Pembroke, whose husband's business interests gave her access to information about household staff throughout the better parts of London.

My dearest Lady Worthington,

I trust this letter finds you in good health. I write to inquire about a matter of some delicacy...

AS SHE CRAFTED HER MESSAGES, Helena reflected on the changes she had witnessed in Edward over the past months. The rakish smile had disappeared, replaced by a brooding intensity that reminded her painfully of their father in his darker moments. Yet beneath the melancholy, she sensed something new in her brother - a depth of feeling, a capacity for love she had never believed him capable of possessing.

Perhaps she had failed him by never demanding more from him, by accepting his casual disregard for others' feelings as simply part of his nature. She had loved him too much, too blindly, allowing him to remain that spoiled boy who believed the world would always bend to his wishes.

But now... now he was learning the hardest lesson of all: that love, *true love*, often meant sacrifice.

The candle on her desk guttered as she sealed her third letter. Outside, darkness had fallen, and she could hear the distant sounds of the household preparing for dinner. Victoria would be waiting in the dining room, her condition now beginning to show beneath her elegant gowns. Poor Victoria, who had gotten everything she thought she wanted, only to find herself married to a man whose heart belonged to another.

Helena pressed her seal into the warm wax, watching as it hardened. She had to believe there was a way to ease this situation, to find some path forward that would bring peace to all concerned. She might have failed Edward in the past by indulging his worst impulses, but she would not fail him now.

Rising from her desk, Helena gathered the letters, ready to have them dispatched first thing in the morning. She paused at her window, looking out at the same view Edward had been contemplating earlier. The autumn wind still rattled the panes, shaking loose the last of the season's leaves from the trees.

CHAPTER THIRTEEN
news beyond these walls

The autumn wind howled against the windowpanes of Blackwood Estate, matching Helena's turbulent thoughts as she sat at her mahogany desk. Her quill scratched across yet another piece of parchment, the ninth inquiry she had written that morning about Charlotte's whereabouts. The steady drip of ink from her pen marked time like a melancholy clock.

Each passing month had brought nothing but silence. Helena's letters, sent to every conceivable contact and acquaintance, returned either unanswered or with disappointing news. The weight of guilt pressed heavily upon her shoulders—guilt for dismissing Charlotte, for believing the worst, for allowing her brother's happiness to slip away.

When Lady Margaret was announced that morning, Helena practically flew from her desk to greet her dearest friend. The two women embraced warmly in the parlor, their separation of a year melting away in the comfort of familiar company.

"My dear Helena," Lady Margaret exclaimed, settling into a plush armchair. "You cannot imagine the sights I've seen! Venice was absolutely magnificent—the gondolas, the masquerade balls, the architecture!"

Helena smiled, genuinely pleased to hear her friend's tales. "Do tell me everything. I've been desperate for news beyond these walls."

"Brussels was simply divine," Lady Margaret continued, fanning herself with an ornate silk fan she'd acquired during her travels. "The architecture! The Grand Place took my breath away with its gilded facades. And the chocolate shops, Helena—you cannot imagine the decadence."

Helena leaned forward in her chair, drinking in every detail of her friend's adventures. Though she maintained her composure, a familiar yearning stirred within her breast. How long had it been since she'd ventured beyond the boundaries of their county, let alone crossed the Channel?

"The Netherlands," Lady Margaret went on, her eyes sparkling with remembered delights, "now there was a revelation. Amsterdam's canals rival Venice's, though in an entirely different way. More orderly, you understand, but no less romantic. And the flowers! Fields of tulips stretching as far as the eye can see, in every color imaginable."

"It sounds absolutely magical," Helena murmured, absently stirring her tea. Her mind wandered to thoughts of freedom, of exploring distant shores without the weight of responsibility that had become her constant companion since George's death.

"You should have seen the merchants at the flower market," Lady Margaret said, reaching for another petit four. "Such characters! One fellow—possessed of the most magnificent mustache I've ever encountered—insisted on teaching me proper Dutch pronunciation. I made an absolute mess of it, naturally, but he was terribly patient."

Helena found herself smiling at the mental image of her perfectly proper friend attempting to wrap her tongue around Dutch consonants. "I cannot picture you massacring any language, Margaret. You were always the accomplished one at school."

"Oh, believe me, I managed it spectacularly." Lady Margaret's laugh tinkled through the room. "But that's half the joy of travel, isn't it? Stepping outside one's comfort and discovering new parts of oneself." She paused, studying Helena's face. "When was the last time you left Blackwood Estate, my dear?"

Helena's fingers tightened imperceptibly around her teacup. "I've been rather occupied with Beatrice's education and Edward's..." she trailed off, unwilling to voice the complications that had arisen since Charlotte's departure.

"Precisely my point," Lady Margaret declared, setting down her fan with purpose. "You've become entirely too absorbed in everyone else's concerns. A change of scene would do you worlds of good. The air in Belgium—there's something different about it. Invigorating. And the society! Such fascinating people one meets while traveling."

"It does sound wonderful," Helena admitted, allowing herself to imagine, just for a moment, what it might be like to break free from the constraints that bound her to Blackwood Estate. The thought of seeing great works of art, of experiencing different cultures, of breathing air untainted by familial obligation sent a thrill through her.

"The museums alone would captivate you for weeks," Lady Margaret continued, warming to her subject. "The Royal Museums of Fine Arts in Brussels house the most extraordinary collection. And the tapestries! My dear, you who have always had such an eye for needlework—you would be in absolute raptures."

Helena's mind wandered to her own modest attempts at embroidery, the few moments of creative expression she allowed herself between managing the household and tending to Beatrice's needs. How different it would be to stand before centuries-old masterpieces, to study the intricate patterns woven by master craftsmen of old.

"The food," Lady Margaret continued, clearly enjoying the effect her tales were having on her friend. "I know you've always appreciated fine cuisine. The pastries, Helena! Light as air and rich as sin. And the chocolate—nothing like that overly sweet confectionery we get here. This is something altogether different, something sublime."

Each description added another layer to Helena's growing sense of wanderlust. She found herself wondering what Beatrice would make of such sights, how her daughter's eyes would light up at the prospect of exploring castle towers and sampling foreign delicacies.

"And the gardens," Lady Margaret added, reaching across to pat Helena's hand. "You who have done such wonders with the grounds here at Blackwood—you would find endless inspiration in the formal gardens of the Low Countries. The precision, the artistry of it all! Every view carefully considered, every path designed to reveal new beauty with each turn."

As they shared tea and cakes, Lady Margaret regaled Helena with stories of her European adventures, while Helena spoke of Beatrice's progress with her new governess and the general goings-on at the estate. Yet beneath their pleasant exchange lay an undercurrent of unspoken matters.

Finally, Lady Margaret set down her teacup with purpose. "Helena, I've news about Miss Larkspur."

Helena's heart quickened. "Charlotte? You've heard something?"

"Indeed. It seems Mrs. Abigail Stahlworth—you remember, the wealthy widow who took her in as a companion—passed away rather suddenly."

"Oh, how dreadful," Helena murmured, genuine sorrow in her voice. Though she had never met the woman, she had been grateful someone had taken Charlotte under their wing.

"That's not all," Lady Margaret continued, leaning forward. "Mrs. Stahlworth left Charlotte an inheritance. A rather substantial one at that."

"An inheritance?" Helena's eyes widened. "How substantial?"

Lady Margaret named a sum that made Helena's teacup clatter against its saucer. "Good heavens! That's more than most peers' younger sons inherit!"

"Indeed. Mrs. Stahlworth had no children of her own, and it seems Charlotte had quite endeared herself to the old woman. But there's more—Charlotte has relocated to Canterbury. She's purchased property near the coast, from what I understand. A modest estate, but quite lovely according to my sources."

Helena sank back in her chair, overwhelmed by this cascade of information. The Charlotte she had known—the quiet, dignified governess who had captured her brother's heart—was now a woman of independent means. The irony of it struck her like a physical blow. Had she known this would come to pass, would she have acted differently? Would she have fought harder to keep Charlotte at Blackwood Estate?

"Canterbury," Helena repeated softly, her mind racing with implications. Edward's anticipation of the birth, constantly sent him away. Yet Helena had watched her brother retreat further into himself with each passing day, his smiles growing more forced, his eyes more distant.

Lady Margaret reached across and squeezed Helena's hand. "I thought you should know. Especially given... well, given everything."

Helena nodded, her thoughts a whirlwind of possibilities and regrets. The wind outside grew stronger, rattling the windows as if nature itself shared her agitation. Charlotte, living independently by the sea, while here at Blackwood Estate, life proceeded along its prescribed path—a path that felt increasingly wrong with each passing day.

"Thank you, Margaret," Helena said at last. "I cannot tell you how much I appreciate you bringing me this news."

The information sat between them like a tangible thing, full of potential and danger in equal measure. What Helena would do with it—what she could do with it—remained to be seen. But for the first time in months, she felt the stirrings of hope, fragile as a spring shoot pushing through frozen ground.

Lady Margaret's eyes sparkled as she leaned forward, her hands animated with excitement. "And speaking of travels, my dear Helena, you simply must hear about my expedition to the Nile. The ancient temples rising from the desert sands like—"

A sharp knock at the door interrupted her tale. Helena turned to see Mary, one of the younger housemaids, hovering in the doorway. The girl's face was unnaturally pale, her hands twisting her apron into knots.

"Begging your pardon, my lady," Mary curtseyed quickly, her voice trembling. "But I must speak with you immediately."

Helena straightened in her chair, noting the obvious distress in the girl's manner. "What is it, Mary?"

"If you please, my lady," Mary glanced nervously at Lady Margaret before continuing, "I was wondering if you might know where His Grace has gone? We've searched the library and his study, but..."

"I'm afraid I haven't seen my brother since breakfast." Helena's brow furrowed. "Is something the matter?"

Mary's fingers worked faster at her apron, the fabric now hopelessly wrinkled. "It's just..." She swallowed hard, her next words tumbling out in a rush. "My lady, you'll need to send Thomas or James for the doctor straight away. The Duchess—she's gone into labor early, and there's blood, *so much blood* everywhere. Mrs. Phillips is with her now, but she says we need a doctor immediately."

Helena shot to her feet, her teacup clattering against its saucer. "Blood? How much blood?"

"It's..." Mary's voice cracked. "It's coating the sheets, my lady. Running down her legs. Mrs. Phillips says she's never seen anything like it."

Lady Margaret gasped softly, her previous animation replaced by grave concern. "Good heavens."

"Send Thomas for Dr. Harrison immediately," Helena commanded, her voice steady despite the fear gripping her heart. "Tell him to spare no expense, to take our fastest horse. And Mary—" She caught the maid's eye. "Have James ride out to search for the Duke. Check the hunting grounds first, then the village. He must be found."

Mary bobbed another quick curtsey before fleeing the room, her footsteps echoing rapidly down the corridor. The sound of shouting and running feet filtered up from below as the household sprang into action.

Helena turned to her friend, who had already risen and was gathering her things. "Margaret, I'm so terribly sorry, but I must—"

"Say no more," Lady Margaret cut her off, squeezing Helena's hand. "Go to her. She needs you now more than I need to tell you about Egypt."

The screams began then—Victoria's voice, high and terrified, piercing through the upper floors of Blackwood Estate. Helena's blood ran cold at the sound. Without another word, she rushed from the room, leaving behind the pleasant afternoon of tea and travel tales, heading toward what she feared might become a tragedy.

epilogue
TEN YEARS LATER

The carriage jostled along the road to Thornfield Academy, the late summer breeze carrying the scent of blooming heather through the window. The Duke of Blackwood, watched his son Nathaniel bounce excitedly on the opposite seat, the boy's dark curls—so like his own—dancing with each movement.

Ten years had passed since Victoria's death during childbirth, leaving Edward to navigate fatherhood alone. The weight of loss had pressed heavily upon him, but Lady Helena's unwavering support had helped him weather the darkest days. Now, as he observed his son's infectious enthusiasm, he felt a bittersweet pride.

"Papa, will there really be other boys my age?" Nathaniel's eyes sparkled with anticipation, so different from his sullen demeanor with his latest governess.

"Indeed, many of them." Edward smiled, remembering his own schoolboy days.

They were to visit each prestigious school in the area, with Thornbury Academy being their first stop on what promised to be an exhaustive journey through London's finest educational institutions. The Duke had carefully selected these establishments, having researched their reputations and academic standards with a thoroughness that would have surprised those who knew only his rakish reputation.

The carriage drew to a halt before an impressive Georgian mansion, its weathered stone walls now housing Canterbury's most prestigious boarding school. Boys in navy uniforms darted across the manicured lawns, their laughter carrying on the wind.

Headmaster Sterling, a distinguished gentleman with silver temples, greeted them at the entrance. "Your Grace, welcome to Thornfield."

Edward's keen eyes swept across the façade of Thornfield Academy, appreciating the classical proportions and elegant symmetry of the Georgian architecture. The morning sun caught the gleam of freshly polished windows, each pane reflecting the verdant grounds beyond. What had once been a nobleman's estate now served a far grander purpose—the education of England's future leaders.

"The east wing was added just three years ago," Headmaster Sterling explained, gesturing toward a seamlessly integrated addition. "We found ourselves quite overwhelmed with applications from London's finest families."

Edward nodded, noting the matching stonework and careful attention to architectural detail. The transformation from private residence to educational institution had been executed with remarkable taste. No expense had been spared in maintaining the property's grandeur while adapting it to its new purpose.

"The grounds are extensive," Sterling continued as they walked along a gravel path. "We encourage physical activity between lessons. A sound mind requires a sound body, as they say."

Young Nathaniel practically vibrated with excitement beside them, his hand clutching Edward's larger one. The boy's enthusiasm both warmed and worried his father's heart. After losing Victoria, Edward had perhaps been too protective, keeping his son close within the confines of Blackwood Estate. But children needed companions their own age—a truth that had become increasingly apparent as Nathaniel grew.

"The dormitories occupy the upper floors," Sterling explained, leading them through massive oak doors into a marble-floored entrance hall. "Each room houses four boys, carefully selected for compatibility in age and temperament."

The interior retained much of its original splendor—ornate plasterwork adorned the ceilings, and rich wood paneling lined the walls. But where formal portraits might once have hung, educational maps and charts now decorated the space. The blend of luxury and learning seemed perfectly calculated to appeal to aristocratic sensibilities.

"Lord Rutherford's oldest boy started with us last term," Sterling mentioned casually. "And the Earl of Pembroke's twins have been here two years now."

Edward recognized the names—all respected peers who had sung Thornfield's praises at various social gatherings. The school's reputation had grown rapidly, attracting the cream of society's young sons. Even the notoriously particular Duchess of Marlborough had placed her grandson in Sterling's care.

Nathaniel tugged at Edward's sleeve, pointing toward a group of boys visible through a window. They appeared to be engaged in some sort of sporting activity, their shouts of excitement carrying faintly through the glass. Edward felt a familiar pang of protective anxiety, even as he acknowledged the necessity of this step.

"Our curriculum is quite comprehensive," Sterling continued, producing a leather-bound prospectus from his coat pocket. "Latin and Greek, naturally, but also modern languages, mathematics, and natural philosophy. We believe in preparing boys for the modern world while maintaining classical standards."

As they proceeded down a wide corridor, Edward observed classes in session through open doors. In one room, boys bent studiously over their work while a master explained geometric principles at a blackboard. In another, a spirited debate appeared to be taking place, with students taking turns standing to present their arguments.

The sight stirred memories of Edward's own education—though his had been conducted by private tutors within Blackwood's walls. He had often felt isolated, particularly after his father's death thrust the responsibilities of the dukedom upon his young shoulders. Perhaps that isolation had contributed to his wilder years, those reckless days before Victoria and fatherhood had sobered him.

"We maintain a strict schedule," Sterling was saying, "but allow ample time for recreation and private study. Structure, we find, provides security for young minds to flourish."

Edward glanced down at Nathaniel, who was drinking in every detail with wide-eyed wonder. The boy had grown so quickly—it seemed only yesterday he had been a squalling infant in his arms, and now here he stood on the threshold of his formal education. Time had slipped past like water through his fingers.

"The library is particularly well-appointed," Sterling said, pushing open another set of heavy doors. "We've made significant investments in expanding our collection."

The room beyond stretched two stories high, with a gallery running around the upper level. Rows of leather-bound volumes lined the walls, their gilded spines catching the light that streamed through tall windows. Several boys sat at long tables, absorbed in their studies under the watchful eye of a librarian.

Nathaniel's grip on Edward's hand tightened, but whether from excitement or apprehension, it was difficult to tell. The magnitude of the change before them settled over father and son like a heavy cloak—the end of one chapter and the beginning of another.

"Perhaps," Sterling suggested, "you'd like to see the dormitory where young Master Nathaniel would be staying?"

Nathaniel tugged at his father's coat sleeve. "Papa, might I explore?"

Edward nodded, watching his son disappear into a group of welcoming boys. "He seems to be adjusting well already."

"Shall we begin the tour of the dormitories, Your Grace?" Sterling gestured toward the grand staircase.

Edward followed Sterling up the grand staircase, his footsteps echoing against the polished wood. Each dormitory they visited revealed the same meticulous standards—four pristine beds with crisp linens, solid oak wardrobes, and well-crafted desks positioned near tall windows to capture the natural light. The brass fixtures gleamed, and not a speck of dust marred the window panes.

Victoria would have approved, Edward thought, running his hand along one of the sturdy bedposts. She had been exacting in her standards, demanding perfection in every aspect of their household. The memory of her fastidious nature brought a sad smile to his lips.

"We ensure each room maintains the highest standards of cleanliness and comfort," Sterling explained, adjusting a slightly crooked picture frame on the wall. "Our housekeeping staff takes great pride in their work."

The attention to detail impressed Edward far more than any ostentatious display of wealth could have. It spoke of genuine care for the students' wellbeing, rather than mere show. *This is what Nathaniel needs—structure, stability, order.*

They moved through several more dormitories, each as immaculate as the last. Edward noted the thoughtful touches in every room—a small shelf for personal belongings, hooks for dressing gowns, even brass nameplates on each bed frame. Sterling explained how roommates were carefully selected based on age and compatibility, with older students often serving as informal mentors to younger ones.

"Your son would be placed here, Your Grace," Sterling indicated a corner room with particularly good light. "The other boys are all from respected families—Lord Pembroke's youngest, Sir William Hayes's son, and young Master Fitzgerald."

Names that would please Helena, Edward mused. His sister had been pushing for this decision for months, insisting that Nathaniel needed companions his own age. The isolation of Blackwood Estate, while safe, had begun to weigh on the boy.

Sterling guided them back downstairs and along a corridor lined with classrooms. Through open doors, Edward glimpsed lessons in progress—a Latin class reciting declensions in unison, a mathematics master demonstrating complex equations, boys bent over maps in geography. The steady hum of learning filled the air.

If only Father could see this, Edward thought. The old duke had insisted on private tutors, believing public education beneath their station. But times were changing, and even the highest ranks of society now saw the value in sending their sons to establishments like Thornfield.

"Our masters are all Cambridge or Oxford educated," Sterling said with quiet pride as they passed another classroom. "We believe in maintaining the highest academic standards while nurturing each boy's individual talents."

The corridor opened into a wider hallway where portraits of previous headmasters hung in gilded frames. Sterling's office lay at the end, its double doors of polished mahogany gleaming in the afternoon light. A brass nameplate declared "Headmaster Sterling" in elegant script.

Edward paused before a particularly fine portrait, studying the stern countenance of a former headmaster. *Would Nathaniel truly flourish here? Or am I merely following society's expectations?* The question that had plagued him for months remained unanswered.

"We understand the gravity of the trust parents place in us," Sterling said softly, noting Edward's contemplative expression. "Every detail of school life is carefully considered with that responsibility in mind."

They continued their tour, Sterling pointing out additional facilities—the infirmary with its resident physician, the music rooms equipped with fine pianos, the art studio flooded with northern light. Each new revelation reinforced the school's commitment to excellence.

Edward found himself increasingly drawn to Sterling's quiet competence and obvious dedication. The man spoke not with the flashy salesmanship Edward had encountered at other schools, but with the measured confidence of someone who truly believed in his mission.

"The previous owner spared no expense in the original construction," Sterling remarked as they approached his office. "We've maintained that standard in all our improvements and additions."

The corridor's walls bore testament to this claim—fine wood paneling below and expertly painted plaster above, with delicate moldings framing each doorway. Even the door handles showed attention to detail, their brass surfaces polished to a mirror shine.

"Would like to meet Mrs. Wordsworth, the proprietress of Thornfield Academy?" Sterling asked, watching the Duke stop dead in his tracks.

Edward's composure wavered slightly at Sterling's mention of a proprietress. "A woman runs Thornfield Academy?" The words escaped before he could temper his surprise.

"Indeed, Your Grace. She purchased the estate several years ago and transformed it into what you see today. Quite remarkable, really. Her vision for education has drawn the finest minds from Oxford and Cambridge to our faculty." Sterling's evident admiration colored his tone. "Would you care to meet her?"

The prospect stirred something in Edward's chest—an inexplicable flutter of anticipation. He hadn't expected this development, and the novelty of it intrigued him. A woman with the means and determination to establish such an institution must be quite extraordinary.

Sterling led them down another corridor, this one broader and more imposing than the others. Tall windows lined one wall, offering sweeping views of the countryside beyond. The afternoon sun streamed through, creating patterns on the polished floor. At the end stood a magnificent door of dark oak, its brass fittings gleaming.

Edward noted that this office, positioned at the heart of the building's original structure, commanded the finest view of the grounds. *A strategic choice,* he thought, allowing its occupant to observe all aspects of school life from this elevated vantage point.

Sterling rapped firmly on the door, then opened it with a slight bow. "After you, Your Grace."

Edward stepped into the room, removing his hat with practiced grace. The office was everything he would expect from someone of refined taste and practical sensibility. Elegant furniture balanced function with beauty, while carefully chosen artwork adorned the walls. But his attention fixed immediately on the figure behind the massive desk in the far corner.

"Forgive the intrusion, Mrs. Wordsworth," Sterling inquired with deference.

"What is it Sterling—"

She sat with her head bent over some papers, a shaft of sunlight catching the familiar chestnut waves of her hair. Edward's heart seemed to stop, then race forward with desperate speed. Even before she looked up, **he knew**—he would have known her anywhere.

The years fell away in that moment, and he was transported back to their last encounter at Blackwood Estate when duty and circumstance had forced them apart. But now, meeting her gaze, he saw not the governess who had captured his heart, but a woman who had forged her own path with remarkable success.

Her face softened, a smile touching her lips that spoke of shared memories and unspoken words. "Your Grace," she said, her voice as melodious as he remembered.

"Wordsworth?" He asked confused, heavy with ten years of regret and wonder.

The air between them crackled with electricity, just as it had in that darkened alcove so long ago. But they were different people now—he a widowed father, she an accomplished woman who had built something extraordinary. The weight of their shared past and separate journeys hung in the air between them, as tangible as the afternoon sunlight streaming through the windows.

Sterling, sensing the charged atmosphere, cleared his throat discreetly. "I'll leave you to discuss the particulars of young Master Nathaniel's education." He backed toward the door, closing it softly behind him.

The door's gentle closure met Charlotte's murmured words, "To command esteem and standing, I adopted the moniker '*Mrs. Wordsworth.*' I never married."

Edward stood transfixed, his hat still in his hands, drinking in the sight of her. Charlotte had aged beautifully, her features more refined, her bearing elegant yet approachable. The years had added character to her beauty, like a fine wine achieving its perfect moment.

"You've built something remarkable here," Edward said softly, his eyes never leaving her face. "Just as remarkable as the woman who created it."

Charlotte's smile bloomed like a flower turning toward the sun. "And you have a son," she replied, her voice warm with sincerity. "I cannot wait to meet him. And, Lady Helena? Beatrice?"

"My sister remarried ... and Beatrice, well, she is a beautiful young lady, eager to enter her first Season," Edward said, wincing at the thought of his niece entering the marriage mart.

"And the Duchess?" Charlotte asked, honestly unaware of the outcome, her hazel eyes reflecting sincere curiosity about the woman who had captured Edward's heart.

"Died... giving birth to Nathaniel," Edward said matter-of-factly, though a flicker of old pain crossed his aristocratic features. The memory of that day still haunted him, though he had trained himself to speak of it without emotion.

"I... I am sorry for your loss," Charlotte said, genuinely, her heart aching for both the motherless child and the man before her. She resisted an urge to reach across the space between them and offer comfort with a touch, knowing such familiarity would be inappropriate.

"Wordsworth," he repeated, savoring the familiar poet's name on his tongue. "It's no wonder I could never find you."

Their bodies moved in perfect synchronization as if the years apart had been mere seconds. Charlotte stepped forward just as Edward strode toward her, their arms finding each other with the familiarity of longtime lovers reunited. The embrace felt like coming home—a sensation neither had experienced since their paths had diverged that fateful day in Hyde Park.

Edward's arms encircled her waist, strong and sure, while Charlotte's hands pressed against his back, feeling the solid warmth of him through his coat. The scent of him—sandalwood and leather—rushed over her senses, exactly as she remembered. Time had not diminished the effect he had on her; if anything, the years had deepened it, like wine aging in a cellar.

Charlotte buried her face in his chest, allowing herself this moment of perfect vulnerability. Gone was the careful facade of the successful headmistress, replaced by the woman who had never stopped loving him. Her fingers clutched at the fabric of his coat, as if afraid he might disappear like a dream upon waking.

Edward's hand moved to cradle the back of her head, his fingers threading through her chestnut waves. The silk of her hair felt the same, the curve of her body against his unchanged. Yet she was different too—stronger, more assured. This was not the young governess he had left behind, but a woman who had built an empire of learning from nothing but determination and vision.

"My Charlotte," he whispered into her hair, his voice rough with emotion. "All this time..."

She lifted her face to his, tears glimmering in her hazel eyes. "Edward," she breathed, and in that single word lay volumes of unspoken feeling—the longing, the regret, the never-ending love that had sustained them both through the long years apart.

Their lips met with the sweetness of a summer rain after drought. The kiss deepened naturally, born of need and memory and the profound recognition that some loves transcend time and circumstance. Edward tasted the salt of her tears, or perhaps they were his own—it hardly mattered. They were together, at last, in this sun-drenched office that represented everything Charlotte had achieved.

When they finally drew apart, it was only far enough to study each other's faces. Edward traced the delicate line of her cheekbone with his thumb, memorizing the subtle changes time had wrought. A few fine lines graced the corners of her eyes now, but they only added character to her beauty. Charlotte's fingers found the silver threading through his temples, a touch both tender and wondering.

This was not an ending, but a beginning—a chance to rewrite their story with the wisdom of experience and the steadfast love that had never died. As they held each other in that moment of perfect understanding, both knew with absolute certainty that this time, *nothing* would tear them apart.

THE END

you might also like
A DARE MAID IN VAIN

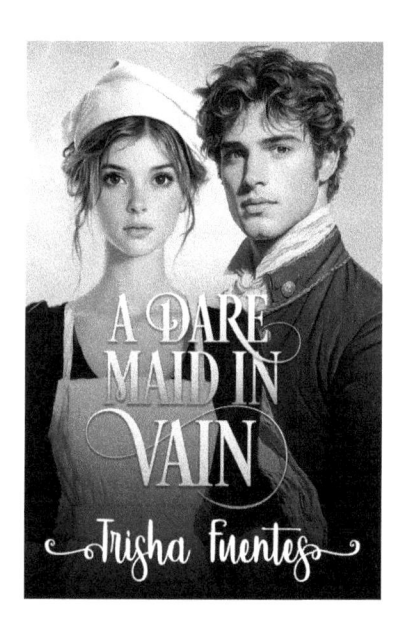

A DARING BET, A STOLEN HEART, AND A LOVE FORBIDDEN BY SOCIETY.

Lady Emily Percy, tired of the monotony of her life, accepts a dare from her naughty friends to elope with the dashing but notorious rake, Lord Edward Grey. However, a twist of fate leads to the wrong woman being whisked away. As Edward realizes his mistake, he falls for the spirited and unconventional lady's maid.

A Standalone Regency Novella

Available in

Ebook & Paperback

best-seller!

A MARRIAGE OF MISMATCH

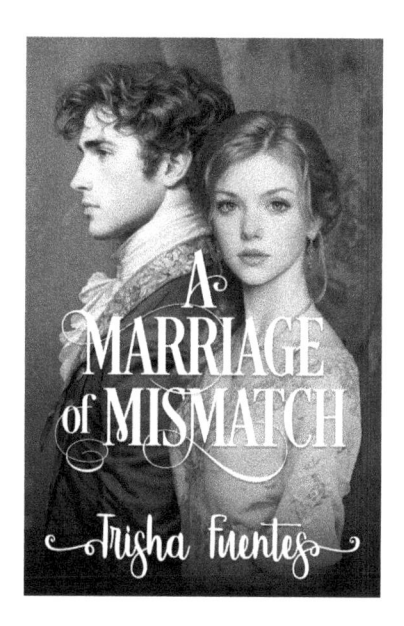

A SCANDALOUS REGENCY ROMANCE

When rebellious Viscount Oliver Thorne is caught in a scandalous situation, his family forces him into a marriage of convenience with the prim and proper Lady Eleanor Cavendish. Oliver is determined to make Eleanor's life miserable, but as they spend more time together, he begins to question his preconceived notions. Will their clashing personalities lead to love or disaster?

Key Features:

- Historical Romance: Immerse yourself in the glamorous world of Regency England.

- Forbidden Love: Explore the tension between a rebellious Viscount and a proper Lady.
- Unexpected Twist: Discover a heartwarming tale of love and redemption.

Get lost in a world of passion, intrigue, and unforgettable characters.

Available in

Ebook & Paperback

one starry night

FATE HAS JOINED THEM TOGETHER, WILL REVENGE OR LOVE BE NEXT?

Miss Charlotte Elkins was the mistress of the Marquess of Harcourt. She had been exclusively his for the past several years. She would have stood by him forever if he hadn't taken a wife without warning. On one starry night, Charlotte sees the Marquess with his wife and is so distraught, runs into the arms of a man with a dangerous past.

Mr. Silas St. Clair was a scandalous rogue. Many ladies had fallen into his trap. Seeing his favorite suddenly wed sends him into a tailspin and into the arms of his competitors mistress.

Read *One Starry Night*, a Standalone Regency Novella!

Available in

ebook & paperback

about trisha

Hey, it's Trish...

I'm a Romance Author of 40+ books, plus a Publishing House Owner of 50+ Pen Name Authors.

I've been writing romance with a whole lot of heat lately. I love to write fun, fast romances with witty leading ladies getting that gorgeous, sexy, yet lovable guy that doesn't take months to finish. Happily Ever After with a little bit of love angst in between. Whether you yearn for Historical or Modern, I always have a story for you!

Rejoice, Romance Reader...

For upcoming releases, book news, and other goodies,

subscribe to my Newsletter!
https://bit.ly/49BR3UB

- instagram.com/authortrish
- amazon.com/Trisha-Fuentes/e/B002BME1MI
- facebook.com/booksbyTrish
- youtube.com/theardentartist

also by trisha fuentes

✻✻ Modern Romance ✻✻

A Sacrifice Play

Faded Dreams

Never Say Forever

✻✻ Historical ✻✻

The Anzan Heir

Magnet & Steele

The Relentless Rogue

One Starry Night

In The Moonlight With You

Captivating the Captain

The Merry Widow

Unrequited Love

The Summer Romance of the Duke

A Dare Maid in Vain

A Marriage of Mismatch

The Spoiled Duke

A Season of Second Chances

❋❋ Series ❋❋

HOLLINGER

Dare To Love - Book 1

A Matchless Match - Book 2

Arrogance & Conceit - Book 3

Impropriety - Book 4

SERVICE•DAUGHTER

The Steward's Daughter - Book 1

The Cook's Daughter - Book 2

The Curator's Daughter - Book 3

THUNDERBOLT

The Surprise Heir - Book 1

A Dance of Deception - Book 2

Win the Heart of a Duchess- Book 3

OBSESSION

Unsuitable Obsession - Part One

Broken Obsession - Part Two

ESCAPE

Swept Away - Book 1

Fire & Rescue - Book 2

The Domain King - Book 3

AGE•GAP•ROMANCE

Whispers of Yesterday - Book 1

His Encore, Her Ecstasy - Book 2

Against the Wind - Book 3

SERIAL•ROMANCE

The Rekindled Flame - Book 1

The Power of Two - Book 2

Facing the Past - Book 3

Taking a Chance - Book 4

Choosing the Future - Book 5

✻

➥**Full Paperback**

https://bit.ly/3XbNK2e